THE JUNIOR LEAGUE

By
Erik Matson

ASTEROID
PUBLISHING
www.asteroidpublishing.com
www.robobattlepets.com

For Tracy, Two-Toe, and Skechers

Illustrations by David White

Book design by Arrow Graphics, Inc.
info@arrow1.com

Printed in the United States of America

First Printing, 2011

Publisher's Cataloging-in-Publication
(Provided by Quality Books, Inc.)

Matson, Erik.
The junior league / by Erik Matson.
p. cm. -- (RoboBattlePets ; bk. 2)
SUMMARY: Three siblings transform their pets into giant battle animals called RoboBattlePets. They join a league in order to compete. The winners will join the military in the battle against the invaders from outer space.
Audience: Ages 7-11.
LCCN 2010910448
ISBN-13: 978-0-9841187-5-5
ISBN-10: 0-9841187-5-6

1. Cyborgs--Juvenile fiction. 2. Pets--Juvenile fiction. 3. Extraterrestrial beings--Juvenile fiction. 4. Human-alien encounters--Juvenile fiction. 5. War stories. 6. Science fiction. 7. Science fiction. [1. Cyborgs--Fiction. 2. Pets--Fiction. 3. Extraterrestrial beings--Fiction. 4. Human-alien encounters--Fiction. 5. War--Fiction. 6. Science fiction.] I. Title. II. Series: Matson, Erik. RoboBattlePets ; 2.

PZ7.M43151Roj 2011 [Fic]
QBI10-600146

Otto Madison lined up RoboCookies in his targeting display and blasted away. His sister Carrie gave a thumbs up as the shots hit their target. He glanced up at the new stadium scoreboard. His points rose as the ion blasts struck home. He looked down and saw that the score on his control panel matched the scoreboard. So far, so good!

The new scoring system calculated points from weapon hits when they were fired in harmless, low-power tournament mode. It had to be working perfectly for the first college RoboBattlePet tournament two weeks from today, so Otto and Carrie were helping their father give it a good test run.

"Hard left, Two-Toe, hard left!" Otto had spent the past week training his cat Two-Toe to make sharp turns on command. Now transformed into a giant armored RoboBattlePet, RoboTwo-Toe swerved sharply to the side, throwing Otto so hard against his shoulder straps that he almost lost his grip on his hand controllers. For this RoboBattlePet design, Otto had added swivel ion cannons, mounted so that he could quickly swing them from side to side while making sharp turns. As his enormous armor-plated cat loped along, Otto swung his cannons around and fired again.

"Yes!" he exclaimed as more points tallied up on the board.

"Slow down, Two-Toe, slow down." His new design and tactics were working great. But to fully test the system, he had to let his sister Carrie score some points too.

Carrie commanded her transmogrified pet hamster, RoboCookies, to chase them. The huge bear-like RoboBattlePet charged, and Carrie fired RoboCookie's phaser blasters as they closed in. Otto watched Carrie's score rise on his control panel as her shots struck RoboTwo-Toe.

"It's working great, Dad," said Carrie over the radio.

"Yeah, watch this," said Otto into his radio headset. "Hard right!" RoboTwo-Toe obeyed, cutting to the right just before RoboCookies could tackle them. Carrie and RoboCookies sped past, and Otto swung his cannons back and carefully aimed at a spot on RoboCookies' rear end that wasn't covered with armor plating. He fired at the unprotected spot, and his points jumped up.

"Nice shot!" laughed his sister Sofie over the radio. She and Dad were watching from the sidelines.

"Close in and grapple," radioed Dad. The scoring system also calculated points from animal strikes and bites but multiplied them by a safety factor so a winning score would be reached before a RoboBattlePet became injured.

"Okay, Dad. Two-Toe, get the mouse!" commanded Otto. RoboTwo-Toe pounced on RoboCookies. The two RoboBattlePets growled and snarled as they grappled. Both of their scores rose as they swatted and nipped at each other. Otto was jostled and tossed backed and forth in his safety harness. It was both scary and exciting to be right in the midst of two wrestling monsters, but he knew he was safe inside his saddle shield.

Otto noticed that the muzzle of one of his ion cannons was jammed into RoboCookies' shoulder between two armor plates. Instinctively, he fired several shots into the unprotected spot, driving his score from 72 to 100. He had won the battle!

"Release!" commanded Otto. Carrie did the same, and the RoboBattlePets separated.

"Otto! We were supposed to be grappling," complained Carrie, brushing her blonde hair out of her eyes.

"Sorry. I couldn't resist," said Otto, feeling a little guilty.

"Actually, that was a good data point," said Dad over the radio. "It demonstrated simultaneous score calculation from biting, striking, *and* weapons fire."

Otto took a deep breath. The musty smell of RoboTwo-Toe and the trampled grass filled his nose. He could feel the giant cat breathing heavily beneath him. It felt great to be on a RoboBattlePet again. Once the RoboBattlePet College League was up and running, Otto and his sisters were going to help organize the Junior League for kids. He couldn't wait!

Otto commanded RoboTwo-Toe back toward Dad and the others on the sidelines. As he rode along, he noticed two soldiers and their military police dogs watching from the sidelines near the parking lot. After the recent attack on Professor Sarah Kyoto's laboratory by the evil Squiddy aliens, the Army had set up a command post at the university. Professor Kyoto had thought it too disruptive for the soldiers to be housed in one of the campus buildings, so the command post was set up in a corner of the school's main parking lot. Because the Squiddies could jam wireless communications, the Army had installed an old-fashioned telephone line that was buried and heavily shielded to protect it from jamming. It connected the command post to the local Army and Air Force bases.

As much fun as he was having, Otto was reminded of the seriousness of their work today when he saw the soldiers. He knew the Squiddies wouldn't give up on trying to stop the

RoboBattlePet project. The ruthless aliens could attack again at any moment. He gave a little shudder and pushed the thought from his mind.

"Great job, children," said Professor Kyoto as Otto and Carrie rode up. She was a pretty Asian woman who wore glasses and a white lab coat. Professor Kyoto ran Centerville University's Alien Technology Research Laboratory and the RoboBattlePet College League. With her was Colonel Daniel Santiago, the commander of the Army's local RoboBattlePet squadron. His short and stocky frame, black crew cut, and military uniform contrasted strongly with the children's father, RoboBattlePet developer Martin Madison, who was tall and slim with blonde hair, and who wore jeans, a button-down shirt, and glasses.

As usual, Dad's attention was focused on his portable computer. Otto's other sister Sofie stood next to Dad with a portable computer of her own. They were comparing results, and her red ponytail bounced as she nodded enthusiastically. A short distance away, a massive orange hermit crab with a giant metallic shell was tasting the weeds growing at the base of the stadium stands. The RoboBattlePet was the transmogrified, or Mogged, form of Sofie's hermit crab Click. Dad had also Mogged their dog Doppler into a gigantic wolf-like RoboBattlePet covered in silver armor plates and equipped with two laser cannons. He sat obediently watching the activities. Dad and RoboDoppler had already done a test battle with Sofie and RoboClick.

"The scoring system is fully functional," said Dad with satisfaction. Colonel Santiago and Professor Kyoto smiled at each other. Dad folded up his computer and slipped it into his pocket. "Looks like we're done for today. Time to de-Mog the RoboBattlePets."

"You mean I don't get to battle Sofie?" asked Otto, disappointed.

"No, not today. But you two can have a battle next time, when we'll be testing the new stadium de-Mogging system."

Dad pulled out one of the remote controls that they used to de-Mog RoboBattlePets. He pointed it at RoboClick, and the giant RoboBattlePet flashed back into a normal little hermit crab. Carrie turned off her saddle shield, unstrapped, and climbed down off of RoboCookies while Dad de-Mogged RoboDoppler, who turned back into a brown and white beagle. Dad pointed the remote a third time, and RoboCookies flashed back into Carrie's black and white hamster Cookies-and-Cream.

Next, it was Otto's turn. A little sad that the day's RoboBattlePet riding was over, he turned off his saddle shield and began unbuckling his safety harness, but paused when a voice he didn't recognize came over the radio. Otto guessed it was one of the soldiers in the command post.

"Colonel, we just got word from Central Command. There's been a saucer sighting, Sector 10, heading 265." The word "saucer" sent a wave of cold fear through Otto's insides.

"Roger that," said Colonel Santiago curtly. "Alpha, Bravo, Charlie, and Delta teams! We have incoming! Double time to the Mog!" The Mog, short for Transmogrifier, was located in Professor Kyoto's laboratory, and was used to transform pets into RoboBattlePets.

The two soldiers on the sidelines began running with their dogs toward Professor Kyoto's laboratory. Two more soldiers and their dogs exited the command post in the distance, also running toward the lab.

Fighting the panic rising inside him, Otto buckled himself back into his harness and turned his saddle's protective force field back on. "Dad! What's going on?" he asked, just as Carrie, Sofie, and their father all began talking over the radio at the same time.

"Everyone, quiet!" ordered Colonel Santiago. "This channel is now reserved for military communications only." He turned to Dad and Professor Kyoto. "You can use the Mog once my soldiers are done." Colonel Santiago then ran off toward the command post.

"Mute your microphones," said Professor Kyoto. Everyone tapped the small headset on his or her ear. Sofie and Carrie picked up Click and Cookies-and-Cream from the grass.

"I want those fighters in the air NOW!" barked Colonel Santiago over the radio.

"Dad, what's the password?" asked Otto anxiously. He

needed it to activate his weapons to full power for fighting the Squiddies.

"M-O-G, Mog," said Dad.

Otto tapped on his control panel's touch screen, navigating through the menus to switch his weapons from Tournament Mode to Full Power.

"Otto, I don't know what's going to happen," said Dad. "If the Squiddies show up, hide. Let the soldiers handle this. Got it?" Otto nodded. The fear in his father's eyes made him *want* to hide.

"Carrie, Sofie, let's go. We've got to get to the Mog and get you back on your RoboBattlePets. Doppler, heel." With that, Dad, Doppler, Carrie, and Sofie ran after Professor Kyoto toward her laboratory. Otto followed them off the field, stopping in the grassy area between the stadium and the lab to wait for the others to return on their RoboBattlePets.

Otto scanned the sky, feeling utterly alone and exposed. Part of him wanted to hide, but another part was annoyed that his dad had told him not to fight the Squiddies. Hadn't he and his sisters proven that they could hold their own in a battle when the Squiddies attacked the last time? Still, Otto felt scared. He knew there was no place safer than on his RoboBattlePet, but he also knew that no one was truly safe when the Squiddies attacked.

Otto waited nervously, fighting to keep his fear under control. He scanned the sky for the Squiddy saucer while his sweaty hands kept a tight grip on his weapons' hand controllers. He wondered if the saucer had already dropped a RoboClone factory just out of sight. Otto scanned the campus for approaching RoboClones, but all was quiet.

Two years ago, the squid-like aliens attacked Earth and almost took over the planet. Using their flying saucers, the Squiddies invaded by dropping house-sized factories: each equipped with a Mog and packed with cloned Earth animals. The Mogs turned the small animal clones into armies of monstrous RoboClones whose deadly robotic weapons attacked every person, vehicle, and building in its path. Nearly half of the world's cities and towns had been completely destroyed by the terrible RoboClones.

The war had seemed hopeless until the Army captured a Mog from a RoboClone factory. Dad figured out how to use it to create the first crude RoboBattlePets, which the Army used to win the war. That Mog now sat in Professor Kyoto's laboratory and was used in her and Dad's research into designing the best RoboBattlePets for fighting the Squiddies. RoboBattlePets looked a lot like RoboClones, but they were created from well-trained pets whose riders controlled them and their weapons. A single soldier on a RoboBattlePet could defeat lots of mindless RoboClones.

After the war, Dad had developed a RoboBattlePet design system that the College League teams were going to use to create RoboBattlePets for their tournaments, with the best RoboBattlePet designs to be adopted by the military to defend the Earth against future Squiddy attacks.

Up until a few months ago, no one knew whether the Squiddies would ever return. But return they did, attacking Professor Kyoto's laboratory with a single RoboClone factory in an attempt to destroy the new RoboBattlePet design system. That also happened to be the day that Otto and his sisters where helping their Dad test the design system, and they were able to use their RoboBattlePets to defeat the RoboClones. Professor

Kyoto had been so impressed that she was going to organize a RoboBattlePet Junior League for kids to compete in.

Otto jumped when two fighter jets screamed low across the sky from behind him. He strained to see if they were chasing a saucer, but all he could see were the jets. Where were the soldiers? What if the Squiddies attacked and RoboTwo-Toe was the only RoboBattlePet ready?

His heart swelled with relief when he saw the first soldier on a RoboBattlePet ride out the large door of Professor Kyoto's laboratory. Through the open door, Otto could see the blue shimmering Mog bubble of the next transforming RoboBattlePet.

The soldier rode up next to Otto. It was Lieutenant Austin. He had fought alongside Otto after the Army showed up near the end of the RoboClone attack on Professor Kyoto's lab a few months ago. His dog had transformed into a giant wolf-like RoboBattlePet whose design was based on one of Dad's earlier designs for RoboDoppler.

"Alpha team Mogged and ready," said the lieutenant into his radio. He turned to Otto. "Don't worry. We'll stop 'em."

Otto nodded, but didn't feel very confident. The Squiddies were intelligent and had likely learned from their past mistakes. He figured they wouldn't simply try to attack the lab with RoboClones again. *But what would they try instead?*

Otto continued scanning the sky as three more soldiers rode out on their RoboBattlePets, each radioing Colonel Santiago, who commanded them to set up a defensive perimeter one hundred meters from the lab entrance.

As the soldiers spread out, Otto considered riding RoboTwo-Toe over to the stands to hide, but something about the soldiers being there made him not want to look scared. Soon Carrie rode out on RoboCookies, followed by Sofie on RoboClick. Professor Kyoto emerged next, riding a giant scorpion-like RoboBattlePet. Finally, Dad rode out on RoboDoppler. All four stopped just outside the door.

Otto saw Colonel Santiago exit the command center. "Otto, join your father," he said over the radio. "Set up a second perimeter half way between my teams and the lab."

Otto tapped his microphone back on. "Okay. I mean, yes, sir. What should we do if they attack?"

"That'll depend on—"

But Colonel Santiago's answer was cut off by painfully loud static over Otto's radio. He ripped the headset from his ear. That had to be Squiddy jamming. They must be close.

"There they are!" Lieutenant Austin pointed toward the horizon past the stadium.

A Squiddy saucer flew in the distance, chased by two fighter jets that were firing their machine guns at it. The jets' glowing tracer rounds bounced harmlessly off of the saucer's invisible force field. Suddenly, the saucer turned and flew straight at the lab.

"Here they come!" yelled Lieutenant Austin.

His heart pounding, Otto lined up the saucer in his targeting display. He wondered if his ion cannons could penetrate the ship's shield.

"Hold your fire!" ordered Colonel Santiago at the top of his voice. "We don't want to hit the jets!"

The Squiddy ship flew over at amazing speed. The jets thundered after it, their machine guns blazing. The roar of the jets made RoboTwo-Toe cower. The three craft climbed high up into the sky, eventually disappearing through the clouds.

Otto realized he was holding his breath. As he let it out, he heard some buzzes from the radio headset in his hand. He slipped the headset back onto his ear.

"Comm check, Charlie team."

"Comm check, Delta team."

"Sir, Central Command is reporting that the jets had to call off pursuit when the alien craft left the atmosphere."

"Roger that." Colonel Santiago checked the clock on his multi-comm as he walked past Otto toward the lab. "Time marked. We'll keep the animals Mogged for one hour—just in case." Otto commanded RoboTwo-Toe to follow the colonel.

"Looks like they're gone," said Colonel Santiago as he reached the others.

"What were they doing?" asked Sofie.

"Probably just testing us," said the colonel.

"Testing us? What do you mean?"

"To see if we have any new defenses in place," explained Dad.

"They're planning their next attack, aren't they?" said Otto, knowing the answer.

"I'm afraid so," said Colonel Santiago.

"Colonel, why were the jets firing?" asked Otto. "Their bullets can't get through the Squiddies' shields, can they?"

"No, they can't," said the colonel. "And the Squiddies' weapons can't fire out when their shields are up either. When they first enter our atmosphere, the Squiddies fly with their shields on so we can't track them on radar. But once they know we've see them, they're no longer worried about being detected. So we fire at them, forcing them to keep their shields up so they can't fire at us."

"Smart," said Otto.

"So what now?" asked Carrie.

"We press on with the RoboBattlePet leagues," said Professor Kyoto, "so that we have the best RoboBattlePets ready when the next attack comes."

"C'mon, let's go!" said Otto impatiently as he and his sisters got off the Electro-bus. "I don't want to miss anything." He looked up at the dark clouds and saw a thin line of blue sky on the horizon, giving him hope that the weather wouldn't cancel the day's tournament.

"Yuck," complained Sofie as she stepped up to her ankle in a mud puddle. Click the hermit crab hung on tightly to Sofie's shoulder as she shook the mud off of her shoe.

"It rained last night," said Carrie. "You should have worn your boots." She was wearing purple rain boots and carrying a matching umbrella. Cookies the hamster rode in Carrie's shirt pocket, his twitching nose sniffing at the smell of popcorn wafting from the stadium. In the spirit of training pets to become RoboBattlePets, Professor Kyoto had encouraged all the spectators to bring their pets along. Sofie had teased Otto that it might help Two-Toe learn not to be such a scaredy-cat.

But there was a better reason Otto and his sisters had brought their pets along. Unlike the recent saucer flyover, the Squiddy RoboClone attack a few months ago had been a terrifying experience that they barely survived. Even though their parents kept telling them not to worry now that the Army was protecting the university, Otto and his sisters had made a secret pact to always keep their pets and RoboBattlePet design cards with them whenever they were near a Mog, just in case the Squiddies attacked again.

They trudged toward the university's sports stadium, which had been completely rebuilt since the last Squiddy attack. The Army had made it a priority to fund its reconstruction so that the RoboBattlePet leagues could get started as soon as possible.

Otto's excitement rose as they drew closer. The new stands were filled with spectators and decorated with balloons and flags. The new scoreboard rose high above the announcer's box at midfield. After helping test the stadium scoring system, they had tested the new de-Mogging system too. It consisted of four transmitter towers set up in the corners of the stadium, and computers in a small, nearby shed. It was used to turn RoboBattlePets back into pets.

Suddenly, the marching band struck up a song, and Two-Toe jumped out of Otto's arms.

"Two-Toe! Stop!" commanded Otto. "Come here, Two-Toe!" The cat slinked back to Otto, eyeing everything suspiciously. "Good boy." Otto bent down and patted Two-Toe, proud of how well trained his cat was. "It's okay, you silly boy, it's just the band."

"Where's Dad?" asked Carrie.

"He should be on the field," said Sofie. "He came early to set up his new Mog."

"There he is," said Otto, pointing. Dad and Doppler were on the field at the nearest end of the stadium, standing next to a machine on a trailer hitched to a pickup truck. As they got closer, Otto saw that it was a mix of human and Squiddy technology. Dad typed on a laptop mounted to one side of the machine. Doppler bounded over to greet them, his tail wagging happily.

"Down, Doppler!" commanded Carrie when the beagle tried to stand up and put his paws on her. Doppler obeyed, and Carrie bent down to pat him. "Good boy. I don't need your muddy paws all over my new shirt."

Several other people were gathered near the new machine. Professor Kyoto and Colonel Santiago were there, plus a man Otto had never seen before. He was tall and heavy-set with a shiny bald head, and he wore an expensive-looking business suit. He chewed on an unlit cigar as he spoke enthusiastically to Professor Kyoto, who looked annoyed.

Otto noticed an older boy leaning against the pickup truck. He looked sort of Middle Eastern with dark hair that was cut in the latest style, and he was dressed like all the cool kids on TV. He was holding the latest multi-comm cell phone that could play the new virtual reality video games. Carrie stared at the boy with a funny look on her face. The boy leaned casually against the truck, trying to look disinterested. But Otto could tell he was watching and listening.

"Hi, Dad!" called Sofie.

"Hey, kids," said Dad looking up. "You're just in time!"

"So this must be the new portable Mog," said Sofie.

"That's right," answered Dad proudly as he inserted a RoboBattlePet design card into a card reader mounted next to the laptop. After extensive research, Dad and Professor Kyoto finally understood Mogs well enough to make a portable one to take outside the lab. Otto was impressed by how much smaller the portable Mog was than the original one from the RoboClone factory.

"We need a better name for it," said Otto. "How about the porta-Mog? Or the mini-Mog?" Dad wrinkled his brow and frowned slightly. Otto looked hopefully to his sisters for support. But Sofie was busy checking out Dad's latest invention, and Carrie was busy pretending not to notice the new boy.

"I call this version the trailer-Mog," said Dad. "I'm currently designing one that fits in a backpack."

"You could really make it that small?" asked Sofie as she ran her hand across a smooth, shiny electronics cover.

The bald man stepped away from Professor Kyoto and came closer, listening intently.

"Of course," said Dad. "The main reason that the factory Mogs are so big is that they are designed to create hundreds of RoboClones as fast as possible. It's simply a matter of heat dissipation and quantum recycling. Theoretically, the Mog could be as small as a wristwatch if you're only transmogrifying a single pet."

"That would be so cool!" exclaimed Otto. He shared knowing looks with Sofie and Carrie. With a Mog that small, they could *always* be ready for a Squiddy attack.

"Yes it would," agreed Dad. "But there's still a lot of SWAP reduction needed to get to that size."

"SWAP?" asked Otto.

"Size, weight, and power," explained Sofie, as if everyone knew that.

"Time to run the diagnostic. Doppler, come here, boy," called Dad as he walked around to the rear of the trailer-Mog. Doppler trotted over. "Sit. Good boy. Now stay." Dad returned to the laptop.

"Everyone, stand back!" called Dad. He tossed a grin at Otto. "What am I supposed to say?"

"Robo-battle-ize!" answered Otto enthusiastically.

"Right. Robo-battle-ize," said Dad with a smile, and he pushed the big red button next to the card reader.

The machine gave off a low humming noise. Doppler froze like a statue as a shimmering blue bubble formed around him. Suddenly, several bolts of electricity sparked and crackled between the Mog and the bubble, making the bald man jump back.

"Whoa!" he yelled, his eyes bulging.

Otto noticed that the crowd in the stands had gone silent. People were standing in their seats and craning their necks to see what was going on. A small crowd gathered around the trailer-Mog as people passing by came closer to get a better look.

As the glowing bubble grew, so did Doppler, morphing into a huge wolf-like animal. Armor plates, sensors, and weapons flashed and shimmered into place all over the RoboBattlePet's body. The bolts of electricity grew more frequent and louder, sending sparks into the air.

But something wasn't right about RoboDoppler. There were way too many weapons and sensors flashing into place. Otto was about to say something when the Mog bubble burst, disappearing in a shower of sparkling lights.

The stadium crowd clapped and cheered. RoboDoppler stood on the muddy grass, struggling under the weight of too many robotic systems. Every type of armor, sensor, and weapon imaginable was piled atop the giant wolf and stuck out in odd directions. The huge dog's legs shook as he tried to take a step forward.

"Dad! What did you do?" asked Sofie, concern in her voice.

"What do you mean?" asked Dad absently as he concentrated intensely on the numbers scrolling by on the laptop's screen.

"That's no way to design a RoboBattlePet!" yelled Otto. He took a few steps toward RoboDoppler, intending to do something to reassure the giant dog. But Otto stopped short, afraid of getting too close to the struggling beast.

"It's a system checkout design," explained Dad as he stared at the laptop. "It tests all the possible Mog functions to make sure the entire system is working properly." Dad waved his hand dismissively. "Don't worry."

"But poor Doppler!" wailed Carrie. "He can't carry all that weight!"

"He'll be fine," Dad assured them. "I just need a few more seconds for the diagnostic program to finish."

RoboDoppler whined and tipped precariously.

"Look out!" yelled Otto, scrambling out of the way.

RoboDoppler roared as he began to fall.

Everyone ran back except Dad, who continued staring at the laptop screen. With a groan of bending metal, RoboDoppler and his tower of robotic systems landed in a large puddle of mud. Dad looked up just as the mud splashed covering his face and glasses.

Dad fumbled to press a yellow button mounted on the trailer-Mog above the laptop. With a flash, RoboDoppler evaporated, leaving Doppler the dog sitting in the mud.

"Well," said Dad, as he squinted at the laptop screen while he cleaned the mud off his glasses with his shirttail. "Everything worked perfectly."

Doppler shook himself, throwing mud everywhere.

"Not everything," said Sofie sarcastically as she wiped mud splatters off of her pants.

The bald man strode forward.

"I have to have this machine," he said. "How much?"

"It's not for sale, Mr. London," said Dad. "My company built this for Professor Kyoto under a government contract."

"I'll pay you double whatever it cost," said Mr. London.

"But it'll be worthless to you without the RoboBattlePet design system," said Dad.

"Then I'll buy one of those too. Money is no object."

"I'm sorry, Mr. London, but the alien technology is restricted to official uses," explained Colonel Santiago firmly.

"I'll call my congressman about that," said Mr. London. "I'm a big campaign contributor." He walked over to Professor Kyoto and the Madison kids.

"Professor, I want to rent this machine from you."

"Mr. London," sighed Professor Kyoto, "our RoboBattlePet research is absolutely critical for the protection of the Earth and the survival of humankind. I realize that the competitions we use to test our students' RoboBattlePet designs also have entertainment value. I also understand that your sports promotion company wants to form a professional RoboBattlePet league. But this is not just a sport to us."

Mr. London looked away impatiently.

"If you start a professional league now," continued Professor Kyoto, "it will draw our most gifted students away from research, and we will end up with RoboBattlePets that are entertaining to watch but useless the next time the Squiddies attack."

Mr. London's eyes lit up as he noticed the Madison kids.

"Say, aren't you those little heroes who fought off the RoboClones?"

"Yes," answered Carrie modestly. The boy leaning against the truck glanced sideways at her.

"That's us!" Sofie said proudly. Otto felt a flush of pride too.

"And we're going to start a Junior League for kids," said Otto eagerly.

"Is that so?" said Mr. London, his eyes narrowing. He turned to Professor Kyoto. "And I suppose this Junior League is going to ensure the survival of mankind?"

"Children often have a closer bond to their pets than adults. It is an active area of research that we are pursuing."

Mr. London rolled his eyes and turned back to the Madison kids.

"Well, kids, my name's Ben London, but everybody calls me Big Ben. I'd like to sponsor your Junior League team. You know, buy you uniforms, water bottles, stuff like that."

"Cool!" said Otto.

"Mr. London—," began Professor Kyoto.

"This is my son Ace," interrupted Mr. London, gesturing for the boy leaning against the truck to come over.

"Hey," said Ace, as he approached.

"Hi," said Carrie.

"You go to my school, don't you?" asked Ace.

"Yeah," answered Carrie. She was in seventh grade at Centerville Junior High. Otto and Sofie were still in grammar school—Otto in fourth grade and Sofie in fifth.

"You're in eighth grade, right?" Carrie asked.

"Yeah," nodded Ace with a smile. "I thought I'd seen you around."

Carrie smiled back, blushing slightly.

Oh great, thought Otto, *Carrie has a crush on him.*

"Ace is going to be in the Junior League," said Mr. London.

"But Dad—," said Ace.

"Mr. London—," tried Professor Kyoto again.

"Ace, now you listen here," continued Mr. London, ignoring Professor Kyoto's attempts to get a word in.

"But, Dad!" complained Ace hotly. "Maybe I don't want to be in the league!"

"You're at least going to give it a try!"

"Mr. London!" said Professor Kyoto in a loud voice.

"What!" demanded Mr. London as he turned to Professor Kyoto, clearly annoyed.

"The tournament is about to start," said Professor Kyoto. "We will have to finish this conversation at another time."

"Fine," said Mr. London curtly. "I'll be in touch." He strode off toward the stands, leaving Ace awkwardly standing there.

Professor Kyoto turned to Ace. "You are welcome to join the Junior League if you'd like, Ace, but you have to be self-motivated and invested in your relationship with your pet."

Ace nodded. "Okay. Thanks."

"Ladies and gentlemen!" boomed the announcer's voice over the stadium's loudspeakers. "Welcome to the first collegiate RoboBattlePet tournament!" The stands erupted into cheers. When the crowd quieted down, the announcer continued. "Today our hometown Centerville University Cougars are hosting the Aggies from the Illinois Agricultural Institute. We'll be starting the competition in ten minutes."

"Kids, run along and watch the tournament while I go clean up," said Dad.

"Let's go," said Otto impatiently. "I want to make sure we get good seats."

"Okay," said Carrie. "But you'd better carry Two-Toe."

Otto bent down and scooped up his cat.

"Enjoy the tournament," said Carrie to Ace as they walked away.

Ace hesitated for a moment, then jumped into stride and caught up with them.

"Sorry about my Dad," said Ace. "He doesn't know when to quit."

"I think Professor Kyoto's advice is good," said Carrie. "You shouldn't join the Junior League if you don't want to."

"That's not it," said Ace. "It sounds cool. I just don't like doing things just because my Dad wants me too. He's got all these big plans about me taking over his business someday. I don't know why he wants me to. Nothing I ever do seems good enough for him."

"That's too bad," said Carrie.

Otto couldn't imagine having a father like that.

Ace shrugged. "Yeah, well, it's okay. He's not around much. He's either working or traveling. My Mom and I hardly ever see him."

"I've got the opposite problem," said Carrie. "My Dad's around all the time. Always inventing stuff in his laboratory in the basement."

"Wacky stuff," Otto added.

"That doesn't sound so bad." Ace looked at Otto with a quizzical grin.

"Let's just say his inventions don't always work quite the way he intends them to." Otto laughed and shook his head. "Especially when he's testing them on us."

"Like what?"

"Like when his self-clearing breakfast table threw our dishes around the kitchen," said Carrie with a grin.

"What about the time when his automatic serving spoons threw mashed potatoes and gravy all over the dining room," said Otto. "Boy, was Mom mad."

"Not half as mad as the time when Dad's self-cleaning toilet turned on while she was sitting on it!" laughed Sofie.

"Yeah," chuckled Otto. "Dad was sure in the dog house after that one."

"Look!" called Sofie suddenly, pointing up into the sky.

Two fighter jets approached in the distance, flying low over the trees. Otto's smile evaporated as the jets thundered over the stadium. He scanned the sky fearfully for Squiddy flying saucers as he clutched Two-Toe. Were the Squiddies about to attack?

"We have to get back to the trailer-Mog," said Otto urgently. He checked his back pocket to make sure his emergency RoboBattlePet card was still there.

"No need to be alarmed folks!" said the announcer in a jovial voice. "That's just our Air Force doing a routine patrol!"

A relieved murmur with some scattered applause rose from the crowd.

"Otto, you're almost as big a scaredy-cat as Two-Toe," laughed Sofie.

Otto felt embarrassed. But he could just imagine the chaos and stampede of spectators if a saucer flew over. They'd never make it to the Mog.

"Why back to the trailer-Mog?" asked Ace.

"Jets chased a Squiddy saucer over the university a few weeks ago," said Carrie as she scanned the sky. "Our dad thinks they're preparing for another attack."

"And when Squiddies attack, you'd rather be inside a saddle shield on a RoboBattlePet than out in the open," explained Otto. "Trust me."

Otto thought back to his dad's plans for a wrist-Mog. If he had one now, then he could stop worrying about being able to reach the trailer-Mog. It would be sort of like having a personal defense shield like in the *Martian Mayhem* video game. As long as he kept his pet, a design card, and a wrist-Mog with him, he'd be ready for anything. What if everyone had a wrist-Mog and was on a RoboBattlePet team—even Mom? They'd all be safer. And if the Army gave out the weapons code during an attack, the Squiddies wouldn't stand a chance!

They made their way along the sidelines toward the stands behind the Cougars' bench. For the first time, Otto noticed all the extra security. There were at least twenty soldiers with military police dogs spread out around the stadium. He was glad they were there but felt annoyed that he had to worry about a Squiddy attack when all he wanted to do was enjoy the tournament.

As they drew near the Cougars' bench, Otto counted a dozen college students wearing red and white jerseys. There were also lots of pets that the team members were going to Mog into RoboBattlePets for the tournament. Otto saw dogs, cats, gerbils, lizards, and a rabbit.

As they surveyed the stands for a place to sit, one of the college girls on the team noticed them.

"Hi, guys!" called the girl and waved. "We saved you some seats right behind our bench!"

"Thanks!" said Carrie as they headed toward the seats. "Good luck today!"

"Why the VIP seats?" asked Ace.

"We've been helping them with their RoboBattlePet designs. I even helped Parker with his," said Otto importantly. "He's the team captain."

"Their uniforms look great," said Carrie. Their padded jerseys had CU on the front for Centerville University and a cougar jumping through the U.

"I hope we get to have cool uniforms in the Junior League," said Otto, remembering what Mr. London had offered. On the other side of the field, the opposing team wore green and yellow uniforms with a white ram's head on the jersey.

"So what are Aggies anyway?" asked Sofie as they sat down in the stands. "Some kind of sheep?"

"No. Aggie is short for Agricultural," explained Carrie. "The students on the other team go to a college where they learn how to raise farm animals. I think that's what they base their RoboBattlePets on."

"I hope somebody uses a pig," said Sofie. "That'd be funny."

"Ladies and gentlemen," boomed the announcer's voice over the loudspeaker. "Today's competition will consist of twelve, one-on-one matchups between team members from the Cougars and the Aggies on their RoboBattlePets. The winner of each one-on-one battle will be decided when the first competitor scores one hundred points. So sit back and enjoy the competition!"

"How do they award the points?" asked Ace.

"For these competitions, they don't use full-power weapons," explained Sofie. "The power's turned way down so it's sort of like laser tag. There are sensors built into the RoboBattlePets that detect when a weapon hits. Those sensors send their data wirelessly to the stadium scoring computer, which calculates what the damage would have been if full-power weapons had been used and then puts that up on the scoreboard."

"Cool," said Ace.

"Yeah, our dad invented it," said Otto proudly. "It takes everything into account: the type of weapon, whether it hits armor or flesh. It even awards points for strikes and bites."

"Speaking of Dad," said Carrie, "here he comes."

Dad drove the pickup truck pulling the trailer-Mog out to the center of the field. Doppler rode in the passenger seat, his head sticking happily out the window. Dad stopped the truck next to a referee dressed in a black and white striped shirt and a black baseball cap. Dad got out of the truck and spoke briefly to the referee, then walked over to the laptop mounted on the side of the trailer-Mog and began typing. The referee blew his whistle.

"Captains!" yelled the referee.

On the sideline in front of them, the Cougar's coach turned around and faced the Cougar bench. He wore a hat with the CU Cougars logo on it and carried a clipboard.

"Parker! Coin toss!" called the coach.

"Right coach." A young African-American man handed his calico cat off to another team member and ran off toward the referee in the middle of the field.

Parker shook hands with the referee and the Aggies' captain, who was a pretty brunette girl.

"I sure hope Parker wins the coin toss," said Otto excitedly.

"What happens when you win the toss?" asked Ace.

"The winner gets to watch the other team captain transmogrify a pet first, and then picks the best RoboBattlePet design to counter it," said Otto. "After that, the teams take turns going first. So it all evens out. Each player gets to bring one pet and an unlimited number of RoboBattlePet designs to choose from. You want to make sure you have designs with different strengths to counter whatever your opponent selects. Each design is loaded on a memory card that stores the evolution and robotic weapons design information that the Mog needs to transform the pet."

"Wow," said Ace. "I didn't realize there was so much strategy involved."

The referee flipped a coin.

"The home team Cougars have won the toss!" said the announcer.

The crowd burst into applause.

"Yes!" yelled Otto as he thrust his fist up into the air. The excitement of the crowd was catching. Scared by the loud crowd, Two-Toe struggled in his other arm. "It's okay Two-Toe," said Otto as he patted the cat to calm him down.

Parker shook hands with the Aggies' captain again and jogged back to the bench.

"First up for the Aggies is Captain Maria Barcelona and her pet calf Joey," boomed the announcer. From the other side of the field, the Aggies' captain led a small brown calf toward the trailer-Mog.

"That calf is so cute," said Carrie.

"Not for long," said Otto. "I can't wait to see her RoboBattlePet design."

Dad showed Maria where to insert her RoboBattlePet memory card. Maria then positioned Joey near one end of the trailer-Mog, stepped back, and pushed the big red button.

The crowd fell silent as the Mog bubble grew around Joey the calf. Spectacular lightning crackled between the trailer-Mog and the bubble. Otto could just make out the tiny calf morphing into a giant bull-shaped RoboBattlePet. Armor plates flashed into place, and weapons shimmered into existence. Suddenly the bubble evaporated, leaving a huge armored bull snorting and pawing the ground. The crowd broke out in applause.

"She made a RoboCattlePet!" laughed Sofie.

RoboJoey's huge horns were both tipped with weapons. One looked like a laser cannon, the other was an ion blaster. A gleaming teardrop-shaped piece of machinery rode on RoboJoey's shoulders. A pair of metal stalks tipped with bug-eyed sensors stuck up from it. A saddle for Maria sat right behind the teardrop sensor pod. Shiny armor plates covered RoboJoey's head, shoulders, and chest, which completed the RoboBattlePet design. Otto guessed that Maria expected RoboJoey to charge headlong at his opponents.

The Aggies' captain climbed up into RoboJoey's saddle. She strapped herself in and activated her saddle shield. The egg-shaped force field shimmered around her for a moment and then became nearly invisible. She urged the giant bull forward and rode toward the Aggies' end of the field.

Back at the Cougars' bench, Parker shuffled through his RoboBattlePet design cards. He selected one and slipped the rest back into his pocket. Parker took his cat from a teammate and headed out to the trailer-Mog.

"He has the sweetest cat," said Carrie. "He's trained him really well."

"I hope he uses his Savannah Tiger 5 design," said Otto. Ace gave him a questioning look. "He needs a large predator—one that evolved to hunt a herd animal like that bull," explained Otto. "The Savannah Tiger 5 looks like a big cheetah and is built for speed."

"And for the Cougars is Captain Parker Greenwood and his cat Patches!" boomed the announcer. The crowd clapped and cheered. Two-Toe tried to squirm out of Otto's arms again.

"That's it," said Otto, "I'm putting you on a leash." Otto pulled one out of his pocket and clipped it to Two-Toe's collar. "I don't want to miss this battle chasing you around."

When Otto looked back up, the Mog bubble was already growing around Patches.

The blue bubble popped into a shower of sparks.

"He *did* pick the Savannah Tiger 5!" said Otto.

Parker climbed up into RoboPatches' saddle and strapped himself in while Dad drove the trailer-Mog off the field. Parker then rode RoboPatches toward the opposite end of the field from Maria and RoboJoey.

"Parker added lightweight flexible body armor so it can still run fast," said Sofie. "He also saved weight by using smaller laser cannons steered by lightweight CCD cameras. They're mounted on quick response turrets."

"The Savannah Tiger 5 may not have as much firepower or defensive armor as other designs," said Otto, "but it makes up for it with agility and speed."

"Don't forget about his net launcher," reminded Sofie. "I can't wait to see that in action!"

"You guys really know this stuff," said Ace, impressed.

"The design system is a lot like a video game," continued Otto. "The evolution simulation is really fun. I like trying different input parameters and seeing how the evolved pet turns out. But my favorite part is adding the weapons and shields. There's a real strategy to matching them to your pet's training and evolution."

Otto had a thought. "Do you like video games?"

"You bet," said Ace.

"Have you beaten the last level of *Scandinavian Smackdown IV?"* asked Otto hopefully.

"Sorry," said Ace, "Haven't played that one."

Otto had been trying to beat that game for months, and he was a little disappointed Ace couldn't give him any tips.

"Ladies and gentlemen," boomed the announcer, "sit back and enjoy the first RoboBattlePet College League battle!"

Otto leaned forward in excited anticipation.

The referee blew his whistle.

The crowd fell silent as Parker and Maria urged their RoboBattlePets toward the center of the field. RoboPatches crept forward slowly, stalking his prey carefully. RoboJoey took a few steps then stopped and pawed the ground, snorting loudly. The huge bull then trotted forward, gathering speed into a full charge. RoboPatches crouched and then also charged.

Otto held his breath along with everyone else as the two RoboBattlePets barreled toward each other.

Parker fired RoboPatches' lasers at the charging bull. Two blasts hit home, tallying a few points on the scoreboard. Maria answered with laser blasts and ion beams of her own, also scoring a few points.

Just when Otto thought the huge bull was about to gore RoboPatches, the giant cat bounded to the right and turned to the side. RoboJoey ran right past the lanky feline, slipping and sliding on the muddy grass as he tried to stop and turn around. RoboPatches' lasers blasted away as the bull slid past, scoring more points on RoboJoey's unprotected rear end.

"Well, that was some move by Greenwood!" called the announcer.

"All right!" cheered Otto with the rest of the crowd.

But RoboJoey was quicker than he looked. Before Parker could react, the bull had charged back at RoboPatches, weapons blazing at close range, scoring more points for Maria. RoboPatches tried to run to the left, but one of the bull's horns caught the cat under a rear leg and flipped him partway up into the air. For a few moments, RoboPatches was running on just his front legs and then fell onto his side.

"But Barcelona answers with a quick move of her own!" the announcer said.

The bull scooped RoboPatches up with his weapon-tipped horns and tossed the cat into the air. But RoboPatches hooked his claws onto the laser cannon mounted on the bull's left horn. And as the giant cat flew up, the weapon ripped loose in a shower of sparks. RoboPatches managed to land on his feet and bound away.

Maria and RoboJoey paused to assess the damage as Parker and RoboPatches ran in a circle around them, lasers still firing and racking up more points. Deciding that she could battle on, Maria commanded RoboJoey to charge RoboPatches a second time.

Again, RoboPatches managed to jump to the side and out of the way. But this time, Parker fired his net cannon. A white net with weights around the edges shot right at the giant bull's head. The net enveloped the bull's horns and tangled his front legs. RoboJoey stumbled and slid in the mud on his front knees, right in front of the Cougar's bench. One of the bull's horns caught in the ground, and the huge bull's rear end flipped up and over his head. As RoboJoey flipped, Maria's saddle shield crashed into the muddy ground with the massive bull's body on top of her.

"Wow!" said the announcer. "Greenwood completely turned the tables on Barcelona!"

Parker stopped RoboPatches to get a better look.

"Are you okay?" shouted Parker.

"I'm fine!" answered a frustrated Maria. "Joey, get up!" The huge bull struggled to regain his footing.

"Well, as long as you're okay," said Parker as he fired a second net onto the struggling bull, followed by a barrage of laser blasts. The points on the Cougar's side of the scoreboard steadily climbed until they reached 100.

"That's the battle!" called the announcer. "Greenwood of the Cougars wins!"

The crowd exploded with cheers and applause. Otto and Sofie exchanged a high five. Otto couldn't believe how awesome that was. The referee ran forward, blowing his whistle and waving his arms. Parker rode RoboPatches back toward the Cougars' end of the field, waving to the cheering crowd as he went. The referee raised a remote and de-Mogged RoboJoey.

Several coaches from the Aggies' bench helped Maria and Joey climb out from under the muddy net.

"That was a fantastic opening match for our first college RoboBattlePet tournament," called the announcer. "Let's give a hand to Maria Barcelona and her calf Joey!" The crowd clapped and cheered as the mud-covered Maria waved and then hugged her muddy calf. Parker had climbed off of RoboPatches and was scratching him under the chin. The referee came over and de-Mogged RoboPatches. The muddy nets flashed away at the same moment. "And congratulations to Parker Madison and his cat Patches!"

"Woo-hoo!" yelled Otto as he clapped along with everyone else. "I can't wait to battle in the Junior League!" Otto gave Two-Toe a big hug. The four kids exchanged smiles.

"So, Ace," began Carrie tentatively. "Do you think you want to be in the Junior League?"

"Will we get to have battles like that?" asked Ace.

"That's the plan."

"Then, absolutely!" Ace's eyes were lit with excitement. "That was too cool."

"Well, the orientation day for the league is next Saturday. If you, ah, give me your contact info, I could e-mail you the information about the sign-up."

"That'd be great."

Both Ace and Carrie pulled out their multi-comms. Carrie fumbled hers and almost dropped it, but she smiled shyly as she held it up. They touched the two small electronic devices together so that they automatically exchanged phone numbers, e-mail addresses, and personal Web pages.

"Is that the new WebTalk 2000?" asked Sofie excitedly.

"Yeah," said Ace in a bored voice.

"Oooh! I want one of those so bad!" said Sofie. "They're really expensive. My dad says I need to save up to pay at least half of it. You must be rich."

"My dad is anyway. Every time he gets a new multi-comm, he buys me the same model," explained Ace. "He jokes that I know how to work them better than he does and that I'll be able to show him how to use it. But he never asks me anything," he said bitterly. "I sometimes feel like I'm just part of his showing off."

"Does he need an apprentice?" asked Sofie. "I'm going to be a business entrepreneur when I grow up."

"Trust me. You do not want to work for my father."

"Maybe not, but I still want a WebTalk 2000."

"The best part is the writing interface," said Ace, slipping his multi-comm back into his pocket. "I do a lot of writing, and the voice-to-text lets me write anywhere."

The marching band suddenly began playing a song. Two-Toe wriggled frantically out of Otto's arms and jumped down through the space between the bleacher bench and footrest.

"Two-Toe!" yelled Otto as his cat dangled by the leash around his neck.

"Let go!" yelled Carrie. "He'll choke!"

Panic tore at Otto as Two-Toe struggled, hanging by the collar around his neck. Otto tried pulling the cat up by the leash, but Two-Toe's head hit the footboard of the stands. Torn between letting his cat choke and letting him get hurt in a fall, Otto let go of the leash, hoping it was true that cats always landed on their feet. Two-Toe fell to the ground below. Without thinking, Otto squeezed himself through the space under his seat and hung by his hands. He looked down to make sure he wouldn't land on Two-Toe, and then let go. The fall was farther than he had expected. His feet hit the ground hard, and he fell on his side.

Otto sat up and looked around. Two-Toe was a few feet away from him, apparently unhurt. The cat was sniffing and batting at something in the weeds. Two-Toe jumped and looked back over his shoulder when Sofie landed next to Otto with a thud.

"Is Two-Toe okay?" she asked. "That first step is a doozy."

"I think so." Otto got up and grabbed Two-Toe's leash. He reached down and patted the cat, who gave a satisfying purr in return. Otto was relieved that Two-Toe was all right. Ever since they fought off the RoboClones together, his bond with the cat was much stronger—Otto didn't know what he would do without Two-Toe.

"Whatcha' got there Two-Toe?" asked Sofie as she went over to see what the cat was playing with. Sofie reached down and picked something up. "Aw, look. Isn't she cute?"

Sofie held up a fuzzy black and brown woolly bear caterpillar in the palm of her hand.

"I think I've found a new pet. I'm going to call her Tracy."

"You pick the weirdest pets," said Otto. "Speaking of which, where's Click?"

"I left her with Carrie," answered Sofie as she stroked Tracy's fur-like hair.

Applause broke out in the stands above them.

"Two-Toe, let's go," said Otto as he pulled on his leash. "We're missing the next battle."

"I'm going to make a RoboBattlePet out of her," said Sofie.

"How are you going to train a caterpillar?"

"Dunno yet." Sofie watched the caterpillar crawl its way up

her arm. "Thing is, I trained a hermit crab, so I bet I can train a caterpillar. Maybe Carrie will have some suggestions."

Otto wasn't sure of the best way to get back to their seats. It was too high to climb back up the way they came down carrying a squirming Two-Toe.

"Looks like we have to go out the back and all the way around," said Otto, and he began to head out toward the open back side of the stands. Suddenly, he heard a familiar nasty laugh and stopped. All his senses went on high alert. He put his arm out and stopped Sofie.

"What is it?" she whispered.

Otto turned his gaze up and toward the rear of the stands, scanning the seats as they sloped up and away. There. He pointed. High up, two teenage boys were climbing down the supports.

"Gimme some!" laughed one of the boys.

"Stop it. You're gonna make me drop 'em," said the boy highest up, who was cradling a cardboard food basket with one arm. "Save some for Randy. He's starving."

Otto's spirits fell. It was Doug and Pete, the best friends of Randy, the bully from Otto's street.

Otto heard a growl in front of them and snapped his gaze down. Sure enough, there stood Randy with his scruffy dog Conan on a leash. Otto's heart began racing. Randy was looking up at Doug and Pete. But Conan stared right at Two-Toe, his teeth bared. Two-Toe arched his back, fluffed up his tail, and hissed at the dog. Conan was nice enough to people and other dogs but hated cats. In the neighborhood, Conan chased Two-Toe every chance he got. Two-Toe hated him.

A mix of fear and anger swirled inside Otto. Randy and his friends were the last kids Otto wanted to meet anywhere, especially here where there were no witnesses. Otto particularly didn't like Randy, a thin and wiry boy with shaggy brown hair and a short temper. Carrie and Randy were in the same class at school and had been friends before the war, but not since. Still, he tended to be on good behavior when she was around. But when she wasn't, Randy could be mean, especially when he got angry.

Doug was a burly, tough-looking boy with curly black hair who played football. His other friend Pete was a tall and lanky boy with sandy hair and freckles and who just seemed to go along with whatever the other two did. When they reached the ground, Randy eagerly accepted the nachos that Doug had no doubt stolen from someone in the stands. Pete glanced in the direction that the growling Conan was staring and saw Sofie and Otto.

"What are you looking at?" challenged Pete, tipping candy into his mouth from a box. All Otto could think about was getting out of there.

"Are you guys stealing food?" accused Sofie, hands on her hips. Randy looked up, wary. But that look vanished as soon as he recognized them.

"Oh, it's just you," said Randy scornfully. "Mind your own business." He dove hungrily into the basket of nachos, acting like he hadn't eaten in days.

"Well, what have we here?" said Doug with a grin. "If it isn't those famous Madison twerps from Randy's street. Do *you* have any snacks you'd like to share with us?" He took a step toward them while Pete chuckled.

"No," said Sofie as both she and Otto took a step back. He looked around for a quick escape.

"Where's Carrie?" asked Randy, frowning slightly.

"Up in the stands, right above us," said Otto, hoping that might offer them some protection.

Randy looked up above them while Conan growled at Two-Toe some more.

"C'mon, let's go," said Randy. "They don't have any food." Randy crumpled the empty cardboard basket and threw it into the weeds. "Those nachos made me thirsty. I need a drink."

"You're gonna need cash for a drink," said Doug. "Maybe they got some." Doug looked at Randy while motioning toward Otto with his head.

"There's a water fountain by the snack shack," said Randy. For a moment, Otto thought they might avoid trouble.

"What? You're not going soft on me are you?"

"Yeah," said Pete. "What's the matter with you?"

Randy looked at Pete, then Doug. He gazed up toward Carrie's seat one more time.

"Hey, Otto," said Randy.

Uh, oh, thought Otto. *Here it comes.*

"How about you lend your old pal Randy some money to buy a soda?"

"No," said Otto firmly, surprising even himself. The other three boys looked surprised. Doug sort of smirked. Otto was scared, but the battle with the RoboClones had taught him that giving in to fear just made things worse.

"What did you say?" said Randy, getting a little angry. "How much money you got? Go on, you know the drill. Empty your pockets."

"No," repeated Otto. His insides churned in turmoil as his hate for Randy began pushing aside his fear.

Randy climbed through the supports separating them and looked down at Otto.

"I said, give me your money." His voice was hard.

"No." Otto felt fear rising in him again as Randy drew close, but he didn't care what happened next. He was done being afraid of this bully. Whatever Randy would do to him, it wouldn't hurt forever.

Anger flashed across Randy's face.

"When I tell you to give me something, you do it!" said Randy loudly.

"And I said no!" yelled Otto defiantly.

Randy lunged at him.

He grabbed Otto in a headlock and dug the knuckles of his free hand into the top of Otto's head. The painful noogies burned Otto's scalp, but the smell of Randy's armpit was worse. Otto gritted his teeth, refusing to give Randy the satisfaction of crying out. The other boys were yelling, egging Randy on. Otto clawed desperately at the arm around his neck, but the older boy was too strong. Randy squeezed tighter, making it hard for Otto to breathe. His situation was looking hopeless. He considered just giving Randy his money.

But if he gave in now, they'd just do the same thing to him

the next time. His only hope lay in making this more trouble than it was worth. He had to keep fighting.

Otto grabbed one of Randy's ankles and pulled it as hard as he could, lifting Randy's foot. Just then, Sofie yelled and jumped on Randy's back. Knocked off balance, Randy fell on top of Otto, elbowing him painfully in the process. Otto kept struggling to get free, ignoring the pain. Doug stepped in and grabbed Sofie's arms from behind, peeling her off of Randy.

Instinctively, Otto swung at Randy's face with his fist. But his punch just grazed Randy's temple.

"Why you little . . . !" said Randy angrily, raising his own fist.

Otto heard the thuds of two people landing in the dirt behind him. He kicked as hard as he could and connected with Randy's stomach just as the older boy punched Otto in the mouth.

"Randy!" yelled Carrie. "What are you doing!"

Randy let go of Otto and rolled away. "Nothin'," he mumbled. "Just having a playful wrestle with my little buddy here." Randy tried to tousle Otto's curly red hair, but Otto snapped his head away.

Otto could feel his lower lip swelling, and he tasted blood. His heart pounded in his chest as hate for Randy swirled in his brain.

Ace took a step toward Doug, who was still holding Sofie's upper arms from behind. Sofie shook his hands off as Otto jumped to his feet.

"They were trying to steal Otto's money!" said Sofie angrily.

"Is that true?" demanded Carrie. Randy stood up and just stared at the ground.

"You don't know the half of it," said Sofie, shaking her head. "They're always picking on Otto and stealing his money and candy."

"So you know these guys?" Ace asked Carrie.

"Who are you?" challenged Doug, looking at Ace.

"Carrie's new boyfriend," said Sofie. By the look on Randy's face, that hurt worse than any of the things Otto wanted to do to Randy right now.

"Sofie!" cried Carrie indignantly.

"Well, he's a boy, and he's your new friend isn't he?" Sofie smirked at Randy.

"I'm Ace. You?"

"Run along, Ace, this doesn't concern you," said Doug, turning his head to spit but not taking his eyes off Ace.

"Right," said Ace sarcastically. "I find a punk like you attacking a little girl, and I'm supposed to just walk away? Why don't you pick on someone your own size?"

"Yeah!" chimed in Otto, happy to have an older boy on his side for once. Though Otto noticed that Doug looked heavier and stronger than Ace.

"Zip it, pipsqueak," warned Randy.

Carrie looked crossly at Randy, who slinked away behind Doug.

"Hey, you're that rich kid!" said Pete.

"Yeah, I suppose I am. And that's why you're the ones who are gonna walk away."

"Oh yeah?" asked Doug. "Why's that?"

"Yeah, why's that?" Pete repeated stupidly. "There's three of us and only one of you."

"Oh, you can count," said Sofie sarcastically. "Your mother must be so proud."

"What you gonna do? Pay someone to fight for ya?" asked Doug. Pete chuckled while Randy stared at his feet.

"You know, I could," said Ace, nodding slightly. "But I have a better idea. Any of you play on a sports team at school?"

"I'm on the football team," said Doug proudly. "What are you gonna do? Challenge us to a football game?" This time, both Randy and Pete snickered.

"No." Ace shook his head. "I'm 'that rich kid' because my Dad's the biggest sports promoter in the tristate area. His donations to our school pay for your football team's uniforms and equipment. And if you guys don't leave, he'll be calling your coach to tell him to cut you from the team."

"No way! Coach would never do that! No matter who your dad is!"

"Well, my dad will only call him because there'll be a certain story about to hit the city news. It'll read something like this: 'The son of sports promoter Big Ben London, at grave risk to himself, stepped in and rescued the young eleven-year-old-heroine of the recent Squiddy RoboClone attack, who was being assaulted by three teenagers under the stands at the RoboBattlePet tournament.' Or something like that. I'll make it good. Your coach will have no choice. He'll just be happy that my dad gave him a heads-up so that he could cut you before the story broke. My dad has lots of contacts in the media. On the right news site, the story might even go nationwide."

"You wouldn't," said Doug, his face white.

"You'd never play on a sports team again," said Ace matter-of-factly.

Otto couldn't believe it. Ace had just defeated Doug without throwing a punch. Otto could almost see steam coming out of Doug's ears as the bully tried to come up with a good comeback.

"Randy," said Carrie quietly. He met her eyes with a strange mix of embarrassment and hope. "You've got a right to be angry about what happened to your dad. But you've got no right to take it out on Otto."

"C'mon," said a dejected Randy, pulling on Doug's arm. "I still want to get something to drink."

Doug glared at Ace for a moment longer and then let Randy pull him away. Pete followed the other two boys.

"That was awesome!" exclaimed Sofie after the three boys left.

"Would you really have done all that?" Otto asked eagerly.

"No," said Ace, smiling sadly. "My dad wouldn't help me. He'd just tell me to fight my own battles, and then turn around and warn me not to get into any fights or do anything else that might bring him bad press."

"How'd you come up with that story?" asked Carrie, not quite sure if it was a good thing.

"I do a lot of creative writing," shrugged Ace. "It's my favorite thing, though my dad thinks it's useless, a waste of time."

"Well, your storytelling came in pretty handy just then," said Otto.

"That was very brave of you," said Carrie.

"To tell you the truth, I was pretty scared there for a moment. But if there's one thing I've learned from my dad, it's how to bluff and play hardball."

"That's two things," corrected Sofie.

"Oh, you can count." said Ace with a teasing smile. "Your mother must be so proud."

It was Friday afternoon—video game time, and Otto was totally in the zone. His thumbs furiously worked the buttons as he rocked the hand controller back and forth.

"Over a hundred kids have signed up for the Junior League so far!" squealed Carrie from where she sat at the family room computer. Otto tried to ignore her and concentrate on beating the last level of *Scandinavian Smackdown IV*.

"That's awesome!" exclaimed Sofie from the floor. She was training Tracy to move on command, using fresh dandelion leaves as a reward.

Sofie and Carrie had helped Professor Kyoto set up the Web site for kids to sign up for the RoboBattlePet Junior League. The first college tournament had been a big success. The Centerville University Cougars had won, and it had been big news on all the Web casts. Since then, the sign-ups had really taken off.

"Otto, did you hear that?" asked Carrie.

"Uh-huh," said Otto absently.

The phone next to the couch rang. "Speaker on," said Sofie. The ringing stopped, and the speaker clicked. "Hello?" she said.

"Uh, hello," answered a nervous boy's voice. "Is this Carrie?"

"No, this is Sofie."

"Oh, uh, this is Randy. Can I talk to Carrie?"

"No," said Sofie. "She said she never wants to speak to you again."

Carrie frowned as she thought for a moment.

"I'm right here, Randy," said Carrie and picked up the phone's handset, which turned off the speaker.

"Hi, Randy," said Carrie coolly. She listened for a moment. Then her voice changed. She sounded confused and concerned. "He did? No, the orientation is still on for tomorrow . . . That's right . . . Have you checked the Web site? . . . Oh, right. Well, it's still on . . . Okay, see you there. Bye." Carrie hung up the phone.

"Don't tell me Randy and his friends want to join the Junior League?" asked Sofie, a note of disgust in her voice.

"Sofie, the league's open to everyone," said Carrie dismissively. "What's strange is that Randy thought the orientation day was cancelled."

"Didn't he check the Web page?" asked Sofie.

"He doesn't have a computer," explained Carrie.

"He doesn't?" Otto thought everyone had a computer these days. "Not even a multi-comm?" Even the most basic cell phones could surf the web.

"No. Remember his dad died in the war?" asked Carrie.

"Yeah," said Otto. That was not something Otto liked to think about. He couldn't imagine losing his father.

"Well, his mom can't work, so they don't have much money," continued Carrie. "They get most of their groceries from charities. So I doubt they can afford a computer."

"So why did Randy think it was cancelled?" asked Sofie.

"Doug and Pete told him."

"Why would they do that?" wondered Otto aloud.

The next morning, the Electro-bus pulled away from the Centerville University bus stop with almost no sound but a whoosh of wind. Carrie dug in her bag. "I can't find my headphones anywhere," she said in frustration.

"Did you leave them on the bus?" asked Dad, watching it disappear in the distance.

"No. I couldn't find them before we left home. I think I may have left them at school."

Carrie led the way on the familiar trek to Professor Kyoto's Alien Technology Research Laboratory. Cookies rode happily on her shoulder, chewing on a sunflower seed. Otto and Dad followed with Two-Toe and Doppler in tow. Sofie brought up the rear, carrying Tracy in one hand. They followed the green signs with arrows pointing the way to Professor Kyoto's laboratory and labeled: RoboBattlePet Junior League Orientation. Unlike their previous visits to the lab, this time the door was wide open, and a sign in the hallway welcomed the Junior League participants.

"Hello, Madisons!" greeted Professor Kyoto enthusiastically from the design computers at the center of the lab.

"Hi, Professor!" said all three kids.

"Good morning, Sarah," said Dad.

"Good morning, Martin. Carrie, do you have the preliminary team rosters?"

"Got 'em right here." Carrie proudly patted her shoulder bag. "I even assigned a parent volunteer as coach for each team." Carrie had been delighted when Professor Kyoto had asked her to help organize the teams.

"When are the other kids supposed to show up?" asked Otto, looking through the doorway at the deserted hallway.

Professor Kyoto checked her watch. "A few minutes ago."

"I wonder where everybody is," said Carrie.

"Yes," said Professor Kyoto, her brow wrinkled. "I was wondering that myself."

"Do you think Doug and Pete told everyone it was cancelled?" asked Sofie.

"I doubt it," said Carrie, though she didn't sound certain.

Great, thought Otto. *Had those jerks ruined the orientation day?*

The five of them waited in silence while Professor Kyoto reviewed the rosters.

A clock ticked on the wall.

Dad checked his watch and looked concerned.

Otto wished he had brought along a video game guide to read. Bored, he looked around and noticed that Carrie was doodling on a pad of paper, drawing little hearts around "Carrie+Ace." Otto was just about to tease her about it when a funny, wide-eyed look came over her face.

"Here comes someone," said Professor Kyoto brightly.

Otto looked toward the door and saw Ace London stroll into the lab with his father. Otto's spirits lifted. He liked Ace. Mr. London's eyes were scanning the lab as if searching for something.

"Hey, Carrie," said Ace. "We must be in the right place."

"Yes," said Carrie brightly, trying to cover up her pad of paper, but she clumsily knocked it to the floor. "You're the first ones here."

"We are? And I thought we were going to be fashionably late. By the way, thanks for the reminder e-mail."

"You're welcome," said Carrie with a nervous smile.

"Hello, Mr. London," said Professor Kyoto. "We didn't expect you here today."

"I just wanted to drop by and see if you had changed your mind about renting that trailer-Mog to me. You could buy a lot of lab equipment with the money I'm willing to pay."

"I'm sorry. I really don't have time to discuss that today."

"Really?" said Mr. London. "It doesn't look too busy around here. I would have thought the place would be crawling with kids by now."

"We were wondering about that too. We are still hopeful that children will be arriving any time now," said Professor Kyoto.

"Wait, don't tell me." Mr. London held up a beefy hand. "You didn't advertise, did you?" He shook his bald head. "No stories on the local news sites, I bet? No human interest spots on the Web casts? Did you even set up a Web page?"

"Actually, we—," Carrie tried to answer, but he cut her off.

"You need my help," said Mr. London, wagging his thick finger at all of them. "I can see that. You're whizzes with all this techno-gadgetry, but you don't know the first thing about promoting a sports league."

"Mr. London—," tried Professor Kyoto.

"Please. Call me Big Ben. Ace has convinced me how important this Junior League is to saving the Earth from the Squiddies."

"I have?" asked Ace, surprised.

"I'd be happy to use my company's resources to promote the Junior League free of charge."

"Well, uh, that's very kind of you," said Professor Kyoto.

"And if enough people get interested in the Junior League," said Sofie, "it'll create demand for your professional league, right?"

Mr. London looked sideways at Sofie. Then he smiled. "You've got quite a little head for business, don't you, my dear?" Sofie smiled proudly. Mr. London continued after a pause. "Yes, that did occur to me. But trust me, that is not why I made the offer."

Mr. London turned to Dad. "So, where's that magical trailer-Mog of yours?"

"Outside, locked in a shed. We won't need it until the first practice."

"Right, of course." Mr. London's eyes looked shiftily around the lab. "Rumor has it that you have the RoboBattlePet design system in here. Mind showing me how it works? Might give me some ideas for promoting the league."

"Of course," said Dad, always eager to show off his inventions. "Right this way."

"Hi, Otto. Hey, Sofie," said Ace. "Those three delinquents leaving you alone?"

As if on cue, in walked Doug, Pete, and Randy.

Otto's mood turned dark. He knew Randy and his friends had signed up, but he had hoped there'd be so many other kids there that he'd easily avoid them. Doug carried a big green bullfrog in a plastic terrarium, and Pete carried a brown rabbit under his arm. Randy brought his dog Conan, of course.

"Welcome," said Professor Kyoto happily. The three boys murmured some hellos. Doug and Pete glowered at Ace. Conan began growling at Two-Toe, who arched his back and hissed at the dog from behind Otto's legs. Doppler took a few steps toward Conan, ready to defend Two-Toe and Otto.

"Heel!" commanded Randy and tugged on Conan's leash. Still, Conan growled quietly. "Hi, Carrie," said Randy.

"Hi, Randy," said Carrie guardedly. "You're some of the first ones here."

Randy pulled something out of his pocket.

"Are these yours?" he asked, holding out some multi-comm headphones.

"Yes!" said Carrie happily. "I've been looking all over for them. Where did you find them?"

"They were left on the school bus yesterday. I thought they might be yours."

"Thanks," said Carrie with a smile and took the headphones. Randy smiled back, but his smile evaporated when he noticed Ace.

"Professor," said Carrie, "this is Randy. He lives on our street. And these are his friends, Doug and Pete."

"Thank you for coming," said Professor Kyoto with a smile.

"We almost didn't," said Doug in an annoyed voice.

"We got that e-mail saying the orientation was off," said Pete, "but then Randy said Carrie told him it was still on. What gives?"

"E-mail?" asked Professor Kyoto.

"Yeah," said Randy. "It looked like it was sent to everyone who registered online."

"I didn't send it," said Carrie to Professor Kyoto.

Mr. London looked over from the design computers.

"So that's why there are so few kids here," he said. "Sounds like someone doesn't want you to start this league."

"I don't think I got that e-mail," said Ace as he pulled out his multi-comm and tapped a few times on its screen. "Nope. Nothing in my e-mail stream."

While everyone stood frowning at each other, two more kids arrived and introduced themselves. A girl named Sunshine came dressed in a t-shirt with a peace symbol, a tie-dyed skirt, and leather sandals, and she wore a hibiscus flower in her long, curly black hair. She had moved to Centerville from Hawaii just before the war. Her pet ferret's name was Ferdinand. She said she hadn't received the e-mail, probably because she only turned on her computer once a week to save energy. The other kid was a boy about a year younger than Otto, short and round with a head full of thick black hair. He had brought a turtle in a cardboard box. Randy and his friends snickered when he told them his name was Bartholomew and that his turtle was named Herschel after a famous astronomer. His family were refugees from an Alaskan Eskimo village destroyed during the war.

"And I *did* get that e-mail," said Bartholomew while Sofie checked out his turtle.

"Really?" asked Dad. "Then why are you here?"

"My spam filter flagged the e-mail as suspicious, and, well, uh, I didn't want to miss a chance to meet Professor Kyoto and see her laboratory. I'm sort of a fan. Scientist of the Year and all that."

"Why, thank you," said Professor Kyoto with a kind smile.

"The little twerp has a crush on the professor!" Doug whispered loudly to Pete and Randy. They all snickered some more. Bartholomew blushed.

"Can you show me that e-mail?" asked Sofie.

"Sure." Bartholomew pulled out his multi-comm and showed it to her.

"Dad, can we use one of the computers?" asked Sofie. "I might be able to figure out where it came from using that e-mail tracing program I wrote last summer at computer camp." Dad agreed, and she and Bartholomew sat down and logged on to his e-mail.

"She can do that?" asked Mr. London, frowning.

"Certainly," said Dad. "It's a fairly straightforward algorithm." Otto came over and watched as Sofie downloaded the program from her personal Web site and launched it. A green line traced a route on a map of Centerville, starting at Bartholomew's house and changing direction at green circles, where network router addresses popped up. Finally, the line stopped at a circle that pulsed on and off. Sofie clicked on it and a window popped up showing more information about the computer at that address.

"The network routing indicates it came from a computer in downtown Centerville, from somewhere inside the Brownstone Office complex."

"Isn't that where your office is?" Ace asked his father.

"Lots of companies have their offices there," said Mr. London dismissively.

"Did you send that e-mail?" accused Ace. "Are you trying to torpedo the Junior League?"

"Me?" asked Mr. London defensively. "You heard the Madison girl. I want the Junior League to succeed. What possible reason would I have to try to stop it?"

Ace stared suspiciously at his father for a moment. "I don't know," he grumbled. "I guess that wouldn't make any sense."

"At least that explains why so few kids are here," Dad said.

"Why would anyone do such a thing?" complained Carrie. "The league is so important for fighting the Squiddies."

"Yeah!" agreed Sofie angrily. "They're like . . . traitors!"

"Could the Squiddies have sent it?" asked Otto.

"I don't think the Squiddies have an office in my building," said Mr. London with a smile, as if he thought Otto was being silly.

"So, what do you think we should do?" Dad asked Professor Kyoto.

She checked her watch. "Let's wait a little longer to see if anyone else arrives."

Three more kids eventually showed up with their pets. The first was a big quiet African-American boy named Darrell who was dressed in overalls and had brought a pet lizard named

Spike. Darrell hadn't received the e-mail. He lived on one of the new farms just outside the city where everything had been destroyed during the war, and they still didn't have Internet or multi-comm coverage.

Right behind Darrell came two girls dressed as cheerleaders. Juanita was a bubbly, pretty girl with straight black hair who cradled in her arms a fluffy grey kitten named Binky. Her "bestest" friend Rava had dark skin and wavy hair in a long ponytail. Rava gave a little wave with a slightly embarrassed look.

Otto recognized her dog as an Akita. Doppler jumped to his feet and the two dogs immediately began sniffing each others' rear ends.

Both girls had come straight from an all-state cheerleading competition. Rava had forgotten her multi-comm at home, and Juanita's battery had run down, so neither had checked her e-mail either.

"Well," said Professor Kyoto, "I'm afraid we're just going to have to reschedule the orientation for next Saturday."

Otto couldn't believe it. He suddenly became very angry at whoever had sent that e-mail. After all the anticipation and build-up, he was going to have to wait another week for the Junior League to start!

"Wait, Professor," said Carrie. "I have an idea!"

"We have enough people here for two teams of six," said Carrie. "We can do a dry run with just the two teams rather than trying to organize a whole league right away. We could even scan the pets today and show everyone how to design RoboBattlePets."

"That's a great idea," said Professor Kyoto.

"I volunteer to coach one of the teams!" blurted Mr. London.

"Why—thank you," said Professor Kyoto, taken aback. "Mr. Madison has already agreed to coach a team with his children on it." Carrie, Sofie, and Otto all smiled at their dad, who smiled back. "So, yes, I guess you can coach the other one."

"Excellent," said Mr. London, clasping his hands together. "I've got big plans! I'm ready to sponsor the team with uniforms, water bottles, and whatever equipment the team needs."

"Cool," said Doug. He turned to Dad. "What about your team?"

"Uh," stammered Dad. Doug sneered slightly. Otto realized his father probably hadn't thought past agreeing to coach.

"Can I be on your team?" Doug asked Mr. London.

"Certainly," said Mr. London with a satisfied smile.

"Me too?" asked Pete.

"Of course."

"What do you think, Randy?" Doug asked.

Randy hesitated and glanced sideways at Carrie. Before Randy answered, Bartholomew spoke up.

"Can I please be on your team?" he asked Dad.

"Sure." Dad smiled. Bartholomew walked over to the Madisons.

"Do you like video games?" asked Otto.

"Like them? I love them!"

"Welcome to the team!" said Otto. "Have you beaten *Scandinavian Smackdown IV* yet?"

"No! I'm still stuck on the Valhalla Lava level."

"C'mon, Randy," urged Doug. Randy looked again at Carrie, who was busy writing down the new team rosters on her clipboard.

"Free cool stuff," added Pete in a sing-song voice.

"Yeah, okay," Randy agreed reluctantly. "I'll be on your team too."

"Welcome to Team London," said Ace's dad and patted Randy and his two friends on the back. "Who else wants to join up with Ace and me?"

Doug and Pete looked at each other, concern and confusion all over their faces.

"Wait?" said Doug to Mr. London. "Ace is on your team?"

"Of course. He's my son."

"You're his dad?" asked Pete stupidly.

"Mr. Madison, I sense you have a good aura," said Sunshine. "Can I please join your team?"

"Of course," said Dad. "Anyone else want to be on our team?"

"I'm afraid one of you will have to join Mr. Madison's team," said Mr. London to Darrell and the two cheerleaders. "To keep the teams even, I only have room for two of you."

"Actually," said Ace, "All three of them can be on your team. I'm joining Mr. Madison's."

"What!" exclaimed Mr. London. "Why?"

"Because you don't know anything about RoboBattlePets. Or coaching!"

"I've worked with lots of coaches," said Mr. London. "It doesn't look difficult—"

"You're only here because you want to start a professional RoboBattlePet league," interrupted Ace. "And somehow this fits into to your plan. Did you even consider what I wanted?"

Otto was shocked at Ace's outburst. He could never imagine talking to his father like that.

"But, but . . ." stammered Mr. London.

Ace turned to Professor Kyoto.

"Can my dad still be a coach even if I'm on Mr. Madison's team?"

"I don't see why not," answered Professor Kyoto slowly.

"Excellent." Ace turned to Bartholomew. "Bart?"

"My name is Bartholomew."

"I know. Can I call you Bart?" asked Ace.

"I guess."

"Why did you want to be on Mr. Madison's team?"

"Because he invented the RoboBattlePet design system. He knows more about creating RoboBattlePets than your father does."

"Exactly!" Ace turned triumphantly to his father. "And that's why I want to be on Mr. Madison's team too. You're always telling me that winning is everything. Well, if I'm going to do this, then I'm in it to win."

Randy and his friends frowned at each other. No one spoke for a moment.

"Well," said Professor Kyoto, trying to sound cheerful, "now that we have our teams, it's time to learn how to make RoboBattlePets. The first step is to scan them. Does everyone have their pets?"

Everyone nodded except for Ace.

"Mine's still outside," he said. "I'll go get it."

Everyone else collected their pets and gathered with Professor Kyoto at the computer that controlled the Scanner.

"Wow!" exclaimed Carrie suddenly.

Otto turned with everyone else to see Ace leading in a beautiful black horse. The horse tossed his mane and whinnied. Ace patted the stallion's muscular neck.

"This is Napoleon," said Ace matter-of-factly.

Randy, Doug, and Pete glowered at Ace as everyone else gathered around his horse. Darrell and Ace discussed horse training while the girls patted Napoleon and told him how beautiful he was.

Professor Kyoto then asked Sofie, Carrie, and Otto to take turns explaining the RoboBattlePet design process. Sofie went first, using Doppler for her demonstration. She showed the new kids how to use the modified Squiddy Scanner to record Doppler's DNA, body structure, and brain connections and how to download the information into the computer. Carrie then demonstrated the evolution program, showing the new kids how to evolve Doppler into a large animal that could carry lots of weapons and shields. She also showed them how to map Doppler's brain connections onto the new RoboBattlePet's brain so that it would remember everything Doppler had been trained to do.

Finally, it was Otto's turn. He demonstrated how to add robotic weapons and shields to complete the RoboBattlePet design. He got lots of questions from the other kids about what it had been like to fire weapons at full power during the battle with the RoboClones.

"I want to be a RoboBattlePet soldier when I grow up," said Doug.

"Yeah," agreed Randy. "We'd get to blow stuff up."

"Yeah," laughed Pete stupidly.

"I'm definitely going to fight the Squiddies the next time they attack," boasted Doug.

"You wouldn't be saying that if you knew what it was really like," said Sofie.

"Being in a real battle is dangerous and scary," said Carrie in a serious voice.

"That's for sure," said Otto, thinking back to how terrifying it had been.

"Maybe for you, pipsqueak," said Doug, who gave Otto a painful flick to the ear. Otto was beginning to dislike Doug almost as much as he disliked Randy.

Professor Kyoto interrupted. "Before we scan everyone's pets, we need to make sure that they are trained well enough to be safe RoboBattlePets. When you are riding them, you will only be able to steer and control them using verbal commands. If you cannot safely control your RoboBattlePet, we will be forced to de-Mog it and have you sit out the rest of practice."

Professor Kyoto set up a test course in the middle of the floor and had the children all get in a line with their pets. One at a time, each of them had to command his or her pet to walk, jump, or crawl out to a cone and back again.

Randy and Bartholomew had some problems, but eventually Conan and Herschel passed their tests. Tracy the caterpillar took forever to round the nearest cone, but passed. Otto was impressed that the pets that Darrell, Rava, and Juanita brought were almost as well-trained as the Madisons'. Doug and Pete, however, just couldn't get their frog and bunny to obey. They yelled and slapped the floor, but their confused pets simply didn't know what they were supposed to do.

Professor Kyoto finally ended the pet testing and continued with her instructions.

"Today we'll still have all of you scan your pets, even if they did not pass the training test." Sofie gave Otto a satisfied look when Doug and Pete both looked down in slight humiliation. "You will then be able to run the evolution simulation and design program from home because we've made them accessible through our Web site. That way you can all spend as much time as you want working on your RoboBattlePet designs. Doug and Pete, you will need to come back after school this week for some basic pet training. Once your pets are ready, we will rescan them so that their new training can become part of your RoboBattlePet design."

Scanning the pets took the rest of the afternoon. While the kids were waiting their turn, Otto answered questions about strategy and design. He also had fun talking to Bartholomew about video games.

When they were done, Professor Kyoto talked to them about safety and reminded them of the importance of being able to control their RoboBattlePets with just verbal commands. She sent them each home with the link to the new Web site for running the evolution and design programs, several blank RoboBattlePet memory cards, and a card writer to connect to their home computer for recording their new RoboBattlePet designs.

"Carrie," said Professor Kyoto as the other kids were leaving, "could you please send an e-mail to the kids and parents who didn't show up today?"

"Sure. What should it say?"

"Let them know that the last e-mail was not from us, that we will have another registration day in three weeks, and that they should check the Web site for status updates."

"Will do," said Carrie.

Over the next week, Otto worked on a new RoboBattlePet design for Two-Toe. He evolved it to hunt polar bears in the Arctic. The resulting cat was large and powerful and had a white coat with light grey stripes. While not as fast over distances as the Savannah Tiger 5 that Parker had used, it was capable of short bursts of tremendous speed and was very strong. Otto hoped that Two-Toe's training to make sharp turns would allow the evolved animal to make fast turns too.

Since the arctic cat was strong and could carry lots of weight, Otto added stainless steel armor plating, which was heavy but gave RoboTwo-Toe maximum protection. On Sofie's suggestion, he picked a version of the armor with a mirror finish that reflected most beam weapons. Otto kept the side-to-side swinging robotic weapon mounts, but replaced the ion cannons he had used to test the scoring system with heavier and more powerful plasma cannons, which were guided by multi-spectral sensors.

Otto named his new design Arctic Panther 1 and saved it to a RoboBattlePet card. He admired the RoboBattlePet image on the card, hoping he'd get to battle Randy and RoboConan during the first team practice.

He was ready!

The morning of the first Junior League practice, Team Madison met at the stadium.

While Dad left to get the trailer-Mog, Otto talked video games with Bartholomew. Carrie, Sofie, and Sunshine took turns riding Ace's horse Napoleon.

"Bart, guess what?" said Otto excitedly. "I finally beat the final boss in *Scandinavian Smackdown IV*!"

"No way! How'd you do it?"

"Well, you know how after you destroy all the Valkyrie Vampires you need to smash the jewel in Odin's forehead?"

"Yeah. But how did you get past his magical shield?"

"Here's the trick: When he's sucking in souls, they pass through his force shield, right? So you switch to your crossbow. And the next time a soul flies through the shield, you fire an arrow at the same spot, and it passes through along with the soul."

"That's awesome!" said Bartholomew.

"My arrow hit him in the chest, and his magical shield turned off. After that, all I had to do was switch to Thor's hammer, double jump up to his head, and smash the jewel!"

"Do you hear music?" asked Sunshine. Everyone looked around.

"Wow, look at them," said Carrie.

Team London came marching up from the parking lot. Pete pushed a cart with a large drink cooler and a boom box blasting music. Everyone wore matching green uniforms with the large white letters BL on the chests. They had green elbow pads, green knee pads, and green water bottles—all with the white BL logo on them. Juanita and Rava were shaking green and white pom-poms and doing cartwheels in unison. Randy and his friends smiled smugly.

"Look at all that stuff," said Otto, feeling a bit envious.

"What does BL stand for?" asked Sofie.

"Ben London," said Ace with a sigh. "That's my father's name and the name of his company. BL is his company logo. But I'm gonna pretend BL stands for Big Losers."

Team Madison cracked up.

"What are you all laughing at?" demanded Mr. London as his team arrived. Clearly, this wasn't the reaction he had been expecting.

"Inside joke," said Ace.

Just then, Dad and Professor Kyoto drove up with the trailer-Mog.

"Welcome, everyone," said Professor Kyoto as she got out. "Are you ready to try out your new RoboBattlePets?" A chorus of yeses rang out from both teams. "After we Mog your pets, we'll start with some riding and target practice. If that goes well, we can try a few practice battles." Everyone exchanged excited grins.

"I want everyone to be very careful today since this will be the first time for most of you riding your RoboBattlePets," continued Professor Kyoto. "The university has graciously agreed to host the Junior League, but we must not abuse that hospitality. In fact, President Providence of the university and Colonel Santiago of the Army have asked to come and watch our first practice. We must be careful not to damage anything and to keep everyone safe."

Dad then pointed out the four de-Mogging towers set up in the corners of the stadium. Each one had an antenna on top.

"Those towers have radars that track the RoboBattlePets within the stadium," explained Dad. He held up his portable computer. "I will be able to track everyone on this display. The towers also have transmitters that can send commands to your RoboBattlePets' onboard computer systems, including de-Mogging commands. If there is a safety issue, I can de-Mog one or more of your RoboBattlePets using my computer."

Dad held up a remote control. "As a backup, Professor Kyoto and I each have one of these. They send the same commands, but only work at close range."

"I suppose that system is not for sale either?" asked Mr. London.

"Correct," said Dad with a smile.

"There are elbow and knee pads in the back of the pickup truck," continued Dad. "Everyone needs to wear them in case your RoboBattlePet de-Mogs while you're riding it because you'll fall to the ground."

"We're all set, thanks," said Randy patting one of his shiny new elbow pads. Doug and Pete smiled smugly.

"So you are," said Dad.

"Nothing but the best for my team," said Mr. London brightly.

Dad reached into the bed of the truck and pulled out an old equipment bag and began handing out pads to Team Madison. Otto looked down at the beat up pads his dad had just given him. They smelled of sweat and dirt.

"Dad, these are disgusting," said Carrie, holding up a particularly nasty elbow pad by her thumb and forefinger.

"They are?" asked Dad, apparently clueless. "Well, they're all we have I'm afraid."

"What we need is a fundraiser," said Sofie as she slipped on the pads. "Then we can buy some new ones."

"Do you all have your pets and memory cards ready?" asked Professor Kyoto. Everyone did. "Excellent. Now remember: Whatever may happen today, this is just a test run. You'll all have plenty of opportunities to improve in the future. Safety is our number one priority."

Dad powered up the trailer-Mog, which gave off a low hum of pent-up electrical power. Professor Kyoto asked Carrie to go first. She inserted her card, placed Cookies on the ground with a sunflower seed, and pushed the big red button. The new kids watched in amazement as the tiny hamster transformed inside the growing blue bubble.

Carrie's improved RoboCookies design used a new evolution that turned her hamster into a huge four-legged animal that looked like a giant ground sloth with a teddy bear face. It had two long saber teeth and pointy claws. Carrie had added lightweight titanium armor and equipped his legs with robotic-powered exoskeletons to make him run faster because the massive animal was naturally slow and lumbering. She completed the design with two rotating phaser blasters mounted on turrets.

Just for fun, she had decorated RoboCookies' chest armor with a jewel-like piece of laser shielding.

Otto went next and yelled, "RoboBattle-ize!" when he pushed the big red button. Soon all the kids were using the catchphrase when it was their turn. One by one the rest of Team Madison brought their pet up to the trailer-Mog, inserted their RoboBattlePet card, and pushed the big red button.

Otto had fun checking out the other kids' RoboBattlePet designs. On his team, Sofie had evolved Tracy into a giant carnivorous silkworm large enough to ride on. She said it could crawl really fast and hunted by shooting silk at giant flying insects that were part of her evolution simulation. RoboTracy had composite armor plating and lots of offensive weaponry, including camera-controlled laser cannons and some cool-looking rocket launchers.

Bartholomew, on the other hand, had opted for a highly defensive strategy. His turtle transformed into a colossal land tortoise covered in armor plating topped with a single rotating ion cannon steered by a laser imaging system.

Sunshine's ferret turned into a cross between a giant ferret and an aardvark with cannons that fired sticky biodegradable foam to immobilize her opponents. Otto didn't give her RoboFerret much chance against some of the other designs. However, its foam cannons could be used at full-strength in tournament mode. That could prove interesting.

Finally, Ace had evolved Napoleon into a horse as big as an elephant. RoboNapoleon was covered in shining armor like a knight's horse from medieval times. He even had a long, pointy disruptor cannon that looked just like a lance for jousting. However, Ace didn't look like a knight when he rode in the saddle. The giant horse was so big that Ace looked like a little kid in comparison.

Next, it was Team London's turn to transmogrify their pets.

Doug's bullfrog Mogged into something that looked like a squat, four-legged dinosaur that Otto had seen in a science documentary. The RoboDino was strong and muscular like its designer. Doug clearly planned on close-in physical battles because most of its armor was near the front, and it only had a single laser cannon for long-range weaponry.

Conan transmogrified into what looked like a huge armor-plated coyote with a net launcher on one shoulder and a swivel-mounted plasma rifle on the other. Darrell's lizard transformed into a beast that looked like a heavily armed wingless dragon. A match between Darrell's RoboLizard and Sofie's RoboTracy would be interesting since both had lots of offensive weaponry.

Pete's bunny turned into a giant rabbit that eerily reminded Otto of the mutant squirrel RoboClones that he and his sisters battled in the last Squiddy attack. It even had the same ion cannon and similar buck teeth but with big floppy ears. The RoboRabbit looked fast and maneuverable.

Juanita's kitten Binky morphed into a beautiful giant panther with long flowing white fur. While the RoboPanther had armor on its head and chest, it had force field generators on the sides and laser cannons pointing forward. Juanita had clearly listened closely to Carrie's accounts of the RoboClone battle and had developed a design that incorporated both force fields and firing weapons.

Rava's dog transmogrified into a snarling, drooling beast that looked to be half-wolverine and half-hippopotamus with a dozen small weapons pointing in all directions. It was pretty ugly. Otto wondered if her strategy was to scare her opponents into submission.

Once all the pets were transmogrified, Dad powered down the trailer-Mog.

In the sudden silence, there was a honking sound, and everyone looked up as a V-shaped flight of geese flew low overhead.

Suddenly, RoboTracy reared up and squirted a rope of silk at the birds. The silk stuck to one of the geese. RoboTracy sucked in the rope as the goose fell from the sky. A moment later the giant caterpillar had the bird in her huge pincers. Everyone watched in stunned silence as RoboTracy chewed up the bird and swallowed it.

Juanita whimpered.

"That poor bird!" wailed Sunshine.

"Sorry!" said Sofie.

"That was so cool!" exclaimed Doug. "Make her do it again!"

"I didn't expect her to do that!" said Sofie desperately. Otto felt badly for Sofie and resolved not to let RoboTwo-Toe try to eat anything he wasn't supposed to.

Professor Kyoto took the opportunity to explain the importance of training their pets to be attentive. "You must also be vigilant about what they might be thinking when they are RoboBattlePets," she added. "And keep them under control at all times." Professor Kyoto then told everyone to mount their RoboBattlePets and fasten their safety harnesses.

"Train your pets well," said Doug quietly in a high singsong voice, making fun of Professor Kyoto. "Control your RoboBattlePet. Eat your vegetables. Don't play with laser detonators." He sneered at Sofie and Otto as they dutifully strapped themselves in.

"Goody Two-Shoes," scoffed Doug. Otto told himself to ignore Doug and focus on controlling RoboTwo-Toe, but he noticed Pete was also not strapping in. Doug and Pete both looked at Randy, who was pulling his shoulder straps on. Randy noticed they were looking at him, stopped, and slowly let his straps fall down unbuckled.

Professor Kyoto started practice by having everyone experiment with riding and steering their RoboBattlePets. Otto let RoboTwo-Toe just run around for a while investigating the other RoboBattlePets but commanded him to turn whenever Otto thought they were too close to one of the others. RoboTwo-Toe seemed particularly interested in RoboCookies, who looked a lot like the polar bears he evolved to hunt. Otto commanded RoboTwo-Toe to turn sharply away from RoboCookies, and they almost ran right into Bartholomew's RoboTurtle who pulled abruptly into his shell.

"Sorry, Bart!" called Otto.

"He keeps doing that," complained Bartholomew. Otto could see Bartholomew needed some advice on how to control his RoboBattlePet better, but that was Carrie's specialty. Otto looked around and found her riding next to Sunshine, coaching her on how to keep her RoboFerret from digging in the stadium grass for food.

Ace was having no trouble with RoboNapoleon, and he and Sofie were lightly sparring without weapons. When RoboTracy reared up and snapped at Ace with her pincers, it reminded Otto of a knight on a horse battling a dragon.

At the other end of the field, Mr. London was yelling at his team.

"You can do better than that, Doug! What if the Squiddies were attacking right now? Rava! Turn faster next time!"

Glad he wasn't on their team, Otto practiced some more hard turns with RoboTwo-Toe but stopped when he noticed that Dad was standing next to Professor Kyoto and pointing to his portable computer's screen. Professor Kyoto nodded, blew her whistle, and motioned for everyone to ride over to them in the middle of the field.

"Children, we need to stop the practice," said Professor Kyoto unexpectedly.

"Stop practice?" Otto echoed, confused.

"Why?" asked Carrie.

"There's a malfunction in the stadium de-Mogging system," answered Dad. "It's not safe to continue practice without a fully operational de-Mogging capability. There's simply too many of you for us to be able to de-Mog with just our remotes. For the moment, we need you to stay right here and keep your RoboBattlePets under control while I try to fix the problem."

A horrible thought struck Otto. "Is it the Squiddies? Maybe their communications jammer affects the de-Mogging system too." An icy silence fell over the group while Dad checked his computer. Otto, Carrie, and Sofie exchanged determined looks. Otto was about to ask for the weapons password, just in case.

"No," said Dad finally. "The wireless network's fine. Based on the error messages, the main computer memory appears to be full. There must be a memory leak." Otto exhaled but scanned the sky for Squiddy saucers, just in case. "Here," said Dad, handing his remote to Mr. London. With that, Dad turned and walked toward the shed that housed the de-Mogging system computers. Doppler followed him dutifully.

"Memory leak?" asked Juanita. "Like, computer chips are falling out?"

"No," laughed Sofie. "It's just an expression. It's a leak of available memory."

Dad, who had been working his portable computer as he walked, bumped painfully into the shed door before opening it.

"What a klutz," said Doug. Sofie shot him an angry look while Pete snickered.

Otto was still confused. "But Dad said the memory's full. Doesn't sound like it's leaking at all."

"Duh," sang Sofie, rolling her eyes. "It's a leak of *empty* memory space. Computer programs are always writing temporary data into memory and then deleting it. If there's a bug so that it doesn't get deleted, then it's like the available memory is leaking away, and the memory fills up. Once the memory's full, the program can't write any more temporary data, so it crashes."

"She's such a nerd," said Doug to Pete.

"I heard that!" said Sofie angrily. Doug and Pete snickered. Doug looked around with a smile.

"Hey, Juanita," he said extra loud, clearly wanting everyone to hear. "You and Rava should have come to the pet-training session with me and Pete. It was awesome. Professor Kyoto videoconferenced in this professional pet trainer from Hollywood who's been helping the college team train their pets."

"Really?" said Juanita, impressed.

"Yeah, we learned a lot. Watch this trick. Skip, up!"

Doug's RoboDino stood up, balanced on his hind legs, and took a couple of jumps like a kangaroo. He came back down, landing right in front of Juanita's RoboPanther. Otto thought the trick was pretty lame.

"Doug, no tricks," warned Professor Kyoto. Doug and Pete shared a mischievous grin. Otto looked away in mild disgust, only to see Carrie flirting with Ace, laughing a little too hard at one of Ace's jokes. Wasn't anyone thinking about the RoboBattlePet practice?

Randy rode up to Carrie. She stopped laughing and looked questioningly at him. "Carrie, I'm, uh, sorry about what happened under the bleachers at the tournament."

"I'm not the one you should be apologizing to," said Carrie tartly and nodded toward Otto. Randy glanced sideways at him.

"Skip, up!" commanded Doug again.

"Doug!" bellowed Mr. London. "Stop horsing around!"

Otto didn't care about any stupid apology from Randy. He was more worried about how RoboConan might react to Doug's reckless antics. Juanita's RoboPanther was moving nervously to the side, while Doug's RoboDino did his hopping trick again. RoboConan was watching the RoboPanther just like Conan did before chasing Two-Toe at home. And Randy had no clue. He was too busy trying to talk to Carrie.

"Randy, you better watch out!" called Otto. But Doug's RoboDino picked that moment to fall back down on all fours, spooking Juanita's RoboPanther. The giant cat darted away, and RoboConan instantly gave chase.

"Help!" yelled a frightened Juanita as her terrified RoboBattlePet sprinted away with RoboConan right on its heels.

"Randy, control your RoboBattlePet!" yelled Professor Kyoto.

"Heel, Conan!" ordered Randy. But the huge coyote didn't stop. "Heel!" Instead, RoboConan chased the terrified RoboPanther back into the rest of the group, right between Doug and Darrell's two RoboBattlePets. One of them snapped at Juanita's RoboPanther as she sped by, the other turned and roared at RoboConan, who skidded to a stop. Randy, who was not strapped in, flew out of his saddle and landed in a heap right between Doug and Darrell's RoboBattlePets.

What happened next happened fast. Otto didn't see all of it because he was busy trying to keep RoboTwo-Toe under control during all the yelling and chaos of roaring and snapping RoboBattlePets. Randy tried desperately to crawl to safety. Mr. London bellowed at the top of his voice, waving his remote crazily while Professor Kyoto ran up pointing hers. She de-Mogged Pete's RoboRabbit before she was knocked to the ground. Somehow, Randy managed to grab the terrified rabbit just as Darrell's RoboLizard tried to eat it.

Mr. London, his arm outstretched, pointed his remote at Darrell's RoboBattlePet. In the same instant that the RoboLizard de-Mogged, RoboConan leapt toward Mr. London, grabbed the remote in his jaws, and wrenched it from Mr. London's grip. Mr. London tripped and fell as RoboConan bounded away playfully toward the end of the field.

Instinctively, Otto urged RoboTwo-Toe toward Mr. London and Professor Kyoto, who were both getting to their feet.

"Are you all right?" asked Otto. Carrie, Sofie, and Ace rode over on their RoboBattlePets too.

"Yes, I'm fine," answered Professor Kyoto as she brushed herself off. Mr. London, on the other hand, was limping on one leg.

"What kind of operation are you running here?" he asked angrily. "My ankle might be broken. And you—" Mr. London pointed a thick finger at Darrell.

"I'm sorry!" cried Darrell, cradling his lizard. "He didn't mean to!"

"We know," said Professor Kyoto firmly. "It was an accident."

"Here," said Randy, handing Pete his bunny. Randy looked over at RoboConan, who had lain down some distance away.

"I dropped my remote," said Professor Kyoto, straightening her glasses as she searched the ground.

"Here it is," said Pete. He picked it up carefully by the edges. Bent and broken, the remote gave off a few feeble sparks.

"It must have been stepped on," said Professor Kyoto as they all looked toward RoboConan. "Randy. I need that other remote. You have to get it from Conan!"

"Right," said Randy, who ran off toward RoboConan.

"Peter, please help Mr. London to the stands." The skinny teenager was not much of a crutch for Mr. London's huge frame as the two hobbled away.

"C'mon, Conan, give me the stick," said Randy, his hand stretched out as he slowly approached the giant armored coyote. "C'mon, boy."

RoboConan watched Randy and wagged his tail playfully. The remote stuck straight up, wedged between his front paws.

Randy almost got close enough to grab it, but RoboConan tilted his head and bit the remote. It splintered in his powerful jaws.

"No!" yelled Professor Kyoto in frustration.

RoboConan jumped up on Randy, knocking him to the ground. The huge dog dropped pieces of the broken remote onto Randy's chest and began licking the boy's face.

"Conan! Stop it!" yelled Randy, raising his arms against RoboConan's giant pink tongue.

"You're ruining everything!" yelled Otto in frustration.

RoboConan looked up at Otto's yell. He saw RoboTwo-Toe and growled threateningly. Suddenly, RoboConan sprinted right at them with a roar.

Before Otto could react, RoboTwo-Toe turned tail and ran. Otto tried to decide what to do as he bounced up and down in his saddle, his shoulder straps keeping him from flying off. He could hear RoboConan barking behind them, closing in. Otto reached down and tapped the green icon on his control panel to activate his saddle shield. The egg-shaped force field shimmered up around him.

Now that he was protected, Otto considered commanding RoboTwo-Toe to stop and fight. If only his weapons were at full power, then he could easily defeat RoboConan. But with his weapons in tournament mode, RoboConan might defeat RoboTwo-Toe and de-Mog him out from under Otto, leaving

Otto exposed to RoboConan's attacks. He decided it was best for now to just let RoboTwo-Toe run.

The giant cat ran straight for the stands below the announcer's box, which rose up above the highest row of seats. With a burst of speed, the giant feline leapt into the stands, scrambling and clawing his way up.

Otto could still hear RoboConan barking behind them and the others yelling in the distance. At the top of the stands, RoboTwo-Toe jumped again, caught the roof of the announcer's box with his front claws, and scrambled up using his rear legs. Otto felt a pang of dread over getting in trouble as siding and shingles flew off the announcer's box.

Once on the roof, RoboTwo-Toe turned, roaring and swatting at RoboConan. The huge dog barked and jumped, trying to reach RoboTwo-Toe from below. More siding flew off every time RoboConan tried to scramble up.

Otto winced every time RoboConan did more damage. They might lose the Junior League over this! Otto wracked his brain for how he could stop RoboConan. He wished he could switch his weapons to full power. But his dad had changed the password for the practice, and Otto didn't know the new one. But then he got an idea. Even in tournament mode, most beam weapons still had some effect at short distances.

"All right, that's it!" muttered Otto angrily. He activated RoboTwo-Toe's automatic targeting cameras and locked them onto RoboConan's head. The next time RoboConan jumped, Otto squeezed his hand controller triggers. The plasma rifles fired, blasting Conan in the face. The reduced-power plasma bolts stung RoboConan's eyes and snout. The huge coyote recoiled backward with a yelp.

RoboConan rubbed his face with a paw and kept his distance. Soon he was barking again, but no longer trying to jump up. That was better. Otto figured they could safely wait it out on the roof until Dad or Professor Kyoto came with another remote and de-Mogged RoboConan.

But RoboTwo-Toe had other plans. Maybe it was all the times Two-Toe had been chased by Conan, or maybe RoboTwo-Toe's evolution made the cat instinctively want to hunt the big coyote. Before Otto could stop him, RoboTwo-Toe leapt off the roof and tackled RoboConan. Biting and scratching, the two RoboBattlePets rolled down the stands. Otto bounced against his shoulder straps, and his saddle shield scraped against the seats as they rolled over and over.

When they hit the ground at the bottom of the stands, the impact separated the two RoboBattlePets. But RoboTwo-Toe hung on to the big dog's net launcher with the claws of an outstretched paw. The launcher ripped off its mount in a shower of sparks. The net launcher misfired, sending a net shooting over RoboConan.

RoboTwo-Toe scrambled to his feet while RoboConan struggled to get from under the net. Sofie, Carrie, Ace, and Sunshine rode up to help.

"Ready, Sunshine?" called Carrie. "Fire!"

Orange foam squirted from the RoboFerret's cannons onto RoboConan. The foam hardened all over the net covering the huge coyote. RoboConan stopped struggling, looking like a giant melting Creamsicle.

"Nice shot!" said Carrie.

"Thanks," said Sunshine. "I hope he's okay under there."

"Stupid dog," said Sofie.

"He's not stupid," defended Carrie. "He's just not well-trained."

Professor Kyoto and Randy jogged over as the rest of the kids gathered their RoboBattlePets around the incapacitated RoboConan.

"Good work," said Professor Kyoto, looking relieved.

"Is he okay?" asked Randy.

"If he's seriously injured, he'll de-Mog on his own," said Professor Kyoto. "If that happens, you'll have to help him get out from under the foam."

"That was quite the tackle," said Ace.

"Thanks," said Otto. "But that was Two-Toe's idea."

"Oh no," said Carrie. "Look at the stands." Not only was the announcer's box torn up, but a trail of splintered seats led down to where they all stood. "Are we going to get in trouble for that?"

Professor Kyoto sighed. "President Providence will not be happy. He just spent a lot of money rebuilding the stadium. But let's not worry about that right now. Can you keep RoboConan here while I retrieve another remote from the laboratory?"

"Sure," said Carrie. "If he tries to get away, Sunshine can squirt him again."

"Look!" said Juanita and pointed. There was movement at the edge of the foam covered net. A paw reached out. Then another. RoboConan struggled to crawl out from under the hardened foam. Otto felt RoboTwo-Toe tense up beneath him, ready to fight.

"The foam hardened on the net, but it didn't stick to Conan!" warned Sofie as RoboConan dragged himself partway out.

"Sunshine, hit him again!" yelled Carrie. Sunshine fired. Some of the new foam stuck to RoboConan's head armor, but most of it just piled up on the grass. With a powerful effort, RoboConan burst free. He nipped viciously at RoboTwo-Toe and then ran off down the field.

"Conan, heel!" yelled Randy, but the giant coyote ignored him and jogged out of the stadium.

"Children!" called Professor Kyoto. "This is very important! Colonel Santiago and President Providence will be here any minute. If we do not get RoboConan under control before they arrive, it jeopardizes the whole Junior League! You must work together, all of you. Try to keep RoboConan from hurting anyone or doing any more damage until I return with a remote. If you can, get him back to the stadium."

She gave Randy a severe look. "And everybody, make sure you are strapped in and your saddle shields are turned on!"

"Let's get him," said Sofie.

"Wait," said Doug. "This is a Team London problem. We'll handle it." He held his hand out to Randy. "C'mon, let's go get your dog." Randy took Doug's hand and climbed up and sat behind Doug's saddle.

"No! This is all our problem," argued Carrie forcefully. "We might lose the Junior League over this! We have to work together."

Randy shook his head. "Doug's right. Conan knows us better. We've got the best chance of controlling him."

"Your dog has already ruined this practice!" yelled Carrie. "I'm not going to let him ruin the whole Junior League!"

"You Team Madison kids had your chance to stop him," said Doug. "Now it's our turn."

Doug rode off with Randy, who wore a pained expression. Juanita and Rava looked at Carrie, then at each other, and commanded their RoboBattlePets to follow Doug.

"This is too important!" yelled Carrie after them. "This isn't about which team is best! This is about the Junior League and defeating the Squiddies!"

"Let 'em go," said Ace. "Randy has a point. Conan does know them best. Let's follow, but hang back." Carrie reluctantly agreed. Otto commanded RoboTwo-Toe to follow with the rest of Team Madison.

RoboConan hadn't gone far. He was digging furiously in the ground next to a small building that housed equipment for taking care of the stadium. Dirt flew back between his legs as he dug.

Team London stopped their RoboBattlePets a dozen yards from RoboConan.

"Let's wait here," suggested Ace. Team Madison stopped a dozen yards away farther still. Otto wondered what Team London's plan was.

He watched as Randy climbed down off of Doug's RoboBattlePet and retrieved a water hose from the wall of the building. The other members of Team London hung back and watched. RoboConan was too busy digging to notice Randy, who tied a lasso loop in the end of the hose. Slowly, carefully, he approached the giant armor-plated coyote.

"Easy, boy," said Randy. RoboConan stopped digging and looked up. "Here, boy." RoboConan came over obediently and tried to lick Randy's face. But Randy sidestepped, threw the hose loop over RoboConan's head, and tightened it gently around his neck. "That's a good boy," said Randy as he scratched the giant dog's ears.

"You got him!" yelled Doug. Randy gave a big smile.

RoboConan looked up and noticed the other Team London RoboBattlePets. Again, RoboConan couldn't help himself and charged right for Juanita's RoboPanther.

"Heel!" yelped Randy as the hose yanked him off his feet. Bouncing and sliding along the ground, Randy tried to let go, but the hose had wrapped around his waist.

"Aah!" yelled Juanita as RoboConan and her RoboPanther locked in a ferocious grapple. As the two RoboBattlePets spun and rolled, Randy flailed about on the hose.

"Attack!" commanded Doug, and his RoboDino lunged at RoboConan from the side, biting down on one side of his saddle. Doug tried firing his laser, but the weak pulses hit RoboConan's flank with no effect. Rava's RoboWolverine joined in on its own and latched onto the other side of RoboConan's saddle with its drooling jaws. RoboConan violently twisted away from Juanita's RoboPanther in an attempt to face his new attackers, and the taut hose flung Randy high up into the air.

The hose, damaged during the fracas, snapped. Randy flew in a graceful arc, crumpling painfully when he hit the ground. The loud creaking of breaking metal cut through the roars and growls as RoboConan's saddle suddenly ripped loose. Free, RoboConan bounded away, leaving Doug and Rava's RoboBattlePets playing tug of war with the saddle. Finally, Doug's RoboDino ripped the saddle away and began chewing on it.

"Are you guys ready to work with us now?" asked Carrie.

"Oh no!" yelled Sofie. "Look!" RoboConan was headed straight for the parking lot where the Centerville University marching band was practicing.

"He might hurt someone!" wailed Carrie.

Otto watched in dread as RoboConan neared the marching band. The color guard were throwing their twirling flags up in the air in unison, like a dozen red and white pinwheels. RoboConan leapt into the air and grabbed one of the flag poles with his jaws. The color guard members screamed and ran in all directions, their flags falling to the ground.

The music abruptly turned to screams and scrambling footsteps as RoboConan bounded among the band members. He growled and shook the flag back and forth as he ran, sending abandoned drums and sousaphones flying through the air.

"Carrie! I have an idea," called Otto. "Maybe I can get him to chase Two-Toe back to the stadium."

"That's worth a try," said Carrie, sounding hopeful.

"Tell the others what I'm doing."

"Okay, but be careful. And try not to hurt Conan."

"Yeah, yeah," mumbled Otto under his breath. If only he could turn his weapons on full power, he'd blast that stupid RoboConan back to normal and this would all be over.

In many video games, the enemies only attacked if you got too close to them. If he got RoboTwo-Toe close enough, maybe RoboConan would decide to chase them again. The trick here would be keeping RoboTwo-Toe from attacking RoboConan first.

"Forward," commanded Otto as he steered RoboTwo-Toe toward RoboConan, who was lying down behind a car and chewing on the flag pole. The huge coyote looked up as they approached. "Hard left," commanded Otto before RoboTwo-Toe and RoboConan could start growling at each other. "Hard left. Stop." RoboTwo-Toe was now facing the stadium. Otto looked over his shoulder. Sure enough, RoboConan had risen to his feet and was staring at RoboTwo-Toe. Otto wished he had a command to make his cat shake his rear end, or do something else to get RoboConan to chase them. "Two-Toe, go forward." RoboTwo-Toe was now walking toward the stadium. That seemed to help. RoboConan took a few steps to follow them. "C'mon," pleaded Otto to himself. He felt a wave of triumph when RoboConan charged at them, barking loudly. Startled, RoboTwo-Toe took off.

Otto held on tight as he bounced up and down in the saddle. When RoboTwo-Toe reached the stadium, they raced past the trailer-Mog. To Otto's relief, there stood Professor Kyoto, pointing a remote directly at them.

But then a horrible thought occurred to him. What if Professor Kyoto accidentally de-Mogged RoboTwo-Toe with RoboConan right behind him?

Otto braced himself for the fall that would come if RoboTwo-Toe de-Mogged.

But it never came. They sprinted past Professor Kyoto, and suddenly RoboConan's deep barking stopped. Otto looked behind him in time to see scruffy little Conan rolling on the grass. They had done it!

"Two-Toe, stop!" commanded Otto. RoboTwo-Toe skidded across the grass and came to a halt. Otto steered him back to Professor Kyoto. The other kids rode up on their RoboBattlePets as well. Randy slipped off the back of Doug's RoboDino while Darrell and Pete came over from the stands carrying their pets and helping the limping Mr. London.

Randy ran over to Conan and hugged him with one arm. He was nursing the other. "Are you okay, boy?" Conan licked Randy's face.

"Professor Kyoto!" called an older grey-haired man from the edge of the parking lot. "We need to talk. Now!"

Uh, oh, thought Otto. *We're in trouble now.*

Professor Kyoto looked torn. Otto braced himself for a fall, fearing that Professor Kyoto would quickly de-Mog the rest of the RoboBattlePets before he and the others had a chance to climb down.

"Stay right here and keep your RoboBattlePets under control while I speak to the president and the band director," said Professor Kyoto. "We will de-Mog them as soon as I get back." She then walked quickly toward the parking lot where Colonel Santiago and the man who must be the university president were talking to a very angry man who Otto guessed was the marching band director.

Just then, Dad and Doppler came out of the shed housing the de-Mogging system computers.

"All set," he said brightly. "I fixed the memory leak and rebooted the system. Shall we get on with practice?"

Carrie explained to Dad what had happened while he was in the shed. In the distance they heard the band director yelling at Professor Kyoto and complaining to the president, who stood glumly with his arms crossed. Professor Kyoto and Colonel Santiago looked grim. His anger vented, the band director returned to helping his students collect their dropped instruments and flags.

President Providence continued speaking with Professor Kyoto and Colonel Santiago. The president wagged his finger angrily at them and shook his head in response to their arguments.

"I wonder what they're saying," said Sofie.

"I dunno, but it doesn't look good," said Ace.

The three adults approached. Otto braced himself for the worst.

"Children," began Professor Kyoto, "I'm afraid I have some very bad news. We won't be having a Junior League after all. I'm sorry." The words hit Otto like a punch in the gut.

"No!" wailed Carrie, who began to cry. She ripped off an elbow pad and threw it angrily at Randy but missed. "This is all your fault!" she yelled. She pulled her other elbow pad off and threw it too, this time hitting Randy's arms as he raised them to protect his face. "You've ruined everything!" Randy looked mortified.

"Nice going, Randy!" yelled Sofie. Randy just looked at his feet.

"I'm sorry, children," said Professor Kyoto. "It's just too dangerous. We are lucky that no one was seriously injured today. I'm afraid we overestimated how responsible children your age are. Many of you have trained your pets well, but some of you have not. A Junior League would simply be too dangerous. I'm also suspending the College League until we have better safeguards in place."

"But we can do better," pleaded Sofie.

"I can help the other kids train their pets," said Carrie desperately. "I'm sure we can train Conan not to chase cats."

"We can also modify our safety protocols," suggested Dad. "In the future we could de-Mog all the RoboBattlePets with our backup remotes if there is a problem with the stadium de-Mogging system."

"Or we can add a backup stadium de-Mogging system," suggested Sofie. "That way, if one has a problem, we'll still have a second one."

"Those are good ideas," said President Providence. "But until they are in place and tested, there will be no college

RoboBattlePet practices or tournaments on this campus. And certainly no Junior League."

Otto was crushed. He couldn't believe it. How were they supposed to help defend against the Squiddies if they couldn't compete their RoboBattlePet designs in the Junior League? Sofie was yelling again at Randy, who turned his back and walked away from the group. Carrie was crying quietly on top of RoboCookies, wiping her eyes on her sleeve.

"Children, dismount your RoboBattlePets," directed Professor Kyoto. "Martin, please de-Mog them." Dad nodded gravely and pulled out his portable computer. He began de-Mogging the remaining RoboBattlePets one at a time, starting with Team London's. It was a grim process. All the kids felt awful about how things had turned out. Dad tapped his computer screen, and the designated RoboBattlePet disappeared in a flash, leaving behind the original pet for its owner to collect. Soon it was Team Madison's turn. Otto climbed down off of RoboTwo-Toe, wondering sadly if he would ever be in a real tournament battle before going to college. Dad de-Mogged Bartholomew's RoboTurtle first, and then Sunshine's RoboFerret.

"Ace, we need to leave," said Mr. London who had limped over from the stands. He was sweating and seemed very agitated. "I need to get my ankle x-rayed."

"We'll do Napoleon next then," said Dad.

Otto noticed a strange sound.

"Dad, wait. What's that noise?" asked Otto, looking around. Everyone went silent and looked at him. A soft humming sound came from the sky. "Does anyone else hear that?"

"Look!" Sofie pointed to the sky over the trees at the far end of the stadium.

A Squiddy spaceship approached in the distance, flying low over the trees. Otto's bitter sadness and disappointment about the Junior League were instantly replaced with mind-numbing terror.

"Get back on your RoboBattlePets!" yelled Dad.

Otto climbed up into RoboTwo-Toe's saddle, activated his shield, and strapped in. He saw that Carrie and Sofie had done the same.

"Ace, we have to leave!" yelled Mr. London desperately. Ace hesitated for a moment but then climbed back onto RoboNapoleon. Otto's heart pounded in his chest as he scanned the sky for more spaceships, but so far it was just the one.

"Get behind the stands!" yelled Professor Kyoto. Everyone began running or riding toward the stands. Everyone except for Colonel Santiago and President Providence. The president stood rooted to the spot next to the trailer-Mog, staring in terror at the approaching saucer. Colonel Santiago pulled desperately on the president's arm, trying to get him to move.

Otto kept RoboTwo-Toe trotting behind the terrified kids running with their pets, instinctively shielding them from the saucer, though he didn't know what the saucer was going to do. Ace and Carrie rode their RoboBattlePets on either side of the group ahead of him. He looked over his shoulder and saw that Sofie had stayed behind with the colonel and the president.

"You guys gotta move!" yelled Sofie. Colonel Santiago looked at her, then up at the approaching Squiddy ship. Finally, he let go of the president. The colonel climbed onboard RoboTracy, sitting just behind Sofie. The Squiddy spaceship came to a hover directly above them, blocking out the sun and casting them in shadow.

"Two-Toe, stop!" commanded Otto, his mind racing. Sofie might need his help.

"President Providence!" called Colonel Santiago as he reached out his hand. "Climb on!" But instead, the panicking president dove underneath the trailer-Mog, trying to hide.

"Forget it! Go!" yelled the colonel as he wrapped both arms around Sofie's saddle shield. Otto could hear Sofie urging RoboTracy forward as fast as possible. As they rode toward Otto, he stared at the huge flying saucer. He'd never been this close to one before. The disk was made of the same purple coral-like material that the Squiddies built all their machines out of. Otto could see three Squiddies floating inside the clear liquid-filled sphere at the center of the ship. They were a strange and terrifying sight. They looked like giant translucent squids with three eyes and lots of long tentacles. As soon as RoboTracy raced past him, he tore his gaze away and turned RoboTwo-Toe to follow them behind the stands.

They found the others hiding there. Dad and Professor Kyoto were trying to calm the terrified kids and their pets. Mr. London sat with his arms around his knees, rocking back and forth, and staring blankly at the ground.

Colonel Santiago slid off of RoboTracy and hurried over to Dad and Professor Kyoto.

"Alpha team, respond! Bravo team, do you read?" called Colonel Santiago into his radio. "Comm's jammed again," he said grimly.

"So is the de-Mogging system," said Dad and folded up his computer. "Sarah, your remote?" Professor Kyoto handed her remote to Dad. He pointed it at the RoboBattlePets and feverishly pushed several buttons.

"Kids!" called Dad. "Your weapons are at full power!"

"Should we fire?" asked Carrie.

"No!" commanded Colonel Santiago. "My soldiers will handle this." He pulled out a whistle and blew it several times. Otto followed the colonel's gaze over to the command post in the parking lot and saw four soldiers hustle out of the door with their dogs. The soldiers stopped for a moment, one of them pointing at the Squiddy saucer. Otto felt a sense of relief that the soldiers would soon be on their RoboBattlePets.

"What are they doing?" said Colonel Santiago to himself. "Get to the Mog!" he shouted and signaled with his hand toward Professor Kyoto's laboratory. But instead, one of the soldiers began running toward the colonel.

Otto wondered why the soldiers weren't trying to Mog their dogs. He also wondered what the Squiddies were up to. He maneuvered RoboTwo-Toe so that he could peer around the corner of the stands and see the spaceship. Sofie rode up next to him.

"Do you see any other ships?" he asked quietly, keeping his eyes on the Squiddy saucer.

"No," said Sofie. "No factories or RoboClones either." Otto felt his initial fear fade a bit. Last time the lone saucer had simply flown away. Carrie and Ace also crowded in behind them on their RoboBattlePets, trying to see what was going on.

"Colonel!" Otto turned. Lieutenant Austin had arrived with his dog.

"Why aren't you in the lab Mogging your dogs?" demanded Colonel Santiago.

"But sir! The lab Mog is down for maintenance. You agreed to let Mr. Madison take it offline since the trailer-Mog was operational."

"Right," said the colonel with a frown, thinking hard as he stared at the Squiddy ship. "We need to drive them away from the trailer-Mog so you can reach it. Have the squad get the anti-tank missiles and the heavy machine gun." Lieutenant Austin sprinted toward the command post.

Otto turned his attention back to the Squiddy ship. Inside the saucer's sphere, one of the Squiddies used its tentacles to move floating colored lights around in the liquid. A cable began lowering a cylindrical pod from the bottom of the ship's purple disk. The pod looked like it was covered in heavy armor plating. The saucer's force field shimmered as the pod reached it. The pod came to a stop a few meters below the saucer and directly above the trailer-Mog.

"They've lowered something from the ship," said Otto. Colonel Santiago, Professor Kyoto, and Dad squeezed passed the other RoboBattlePets to stand next to RoboTwo-Toe to see.

Suddenly, a cone of sparkling green light shot down from the pod, covering the trailer-Mog and the grass around it.

"What's that?" asked Sofie.

"No idea," said the colonel. "But they must have turned off their shields to lower it. If so, our weapons should be able to take out the saucer."

"What about the president?" asked Professor Kyoto.

"Hopefully, the trailer-Mog will protect him," said the colonel.

Eight soldiers arrived carrying shoulder-launched missiles, a tripod-mounted machine gun, and several belts of ammo. They also had their dogs with them.

"Set up over there." Colonel Santiago pointed to a groundskeeping shed. "Use that building for cover." The soldiers hustled away with their weapons, except for Lieutenant Austin, who held the leashes of all eight dogs. Otto found it comforting that the soldiers were in charge.

"Look at that," said Ace. The trailer-Mog shifted and began to rise slowly into the air. The terrified president lay curled up on the grass underneath. "What are they doing?"

"Looks like they're trying to steal the trailer-Mog," said Sofie.

"But why?" asked Carrie.

"They probably want to figure out how to disable it," said Colonel Santiago.

"When the Squiddies left after the war, they sent a remote command that disabled all the factory Mogs they left behind," said Professor Kyoto.

"It took us several months to figure out a way to reactivate them," said Dad. "Perhaps they want to understand how we did it."

"Capture your enemy's technology, and reverse engineer it," said Colonel Santiago. "That's exactly what we did to them. If they understand how our technology works, they may be able to find a vulnerability to exploit."

"They're ready, sir," said Lieutenant Austin.

Colonel Santiago ran over to his soldiers behind the shed.

"Fire!" he commanded.

Chapter 21

A barrage of missiles and machine gun bullets shot out at the saucer.

But the barrage exploded harmlessly on the saucer's force field. Otto's spirits fell. The colonel had been wrong. The Squddies hadn't turned off their ship's force field. Somehow, they had lowered the pod through it.

A glowing red spot appeared on the side of the pod. Suddenly, a red energy beam shot out from the spot. The shed exploded, throwing soldiers and their weapons in all directions.

Otto was stunned. The Army's squadron had been knocked out of commission by a single shot!

"Everyone, get back!" shouted Professor Kyoto as she pulled Dad back with her behind the stands. Otto commanded RoboTwo-Toe to back up a little, but he still kept an eye on the saucer. Colonel Santiago and four of his soldiers dragged their three wounded behind the stands.

"Colonel, what do we do now?" asked Lieutenant Austin.

"How long would it take to get the Mog in the lab back online?" Colonel Santiago asked Dad.

"The transduction power inverters are completely disassembled. An hour—at least."

"Then we wait," said the colonel. "My men got a call through to the Air Force. Jet fighters are on the way."

"So we just let them take the trailer-Mog?" asked Dad.

"You saw what they did to that shed," said Professor Kyoto, her voice rising in pitch. "We can't risk drawing their fire. We have children back here!"

"She's right," said Colonel Santiago. "Our best option is to wait it out."

"But they might be able to figure out how to keep us from making more RoboBattlePets," argued Otto. "You know, with a jammer or something."

"Perhaps," said Professor Kyoto. "But we would be able to shield our Mogs from any jamming signal, wouldn't we Martin?"

"In theory," said Dad, his eyebrows scrunched up in thought. "This may be just what the colonel suggests. A fishing expedition to see if they can find anything that would help them . . ." Dad's voice trailed off.

"Colonel!" said Dad suddenly and forcefully. "We have to stop them!" Otto looked at his Dad. He was white in the face and wide-eyed as he grabbed Colonel Santiago by the arm. "It's absolutely critical that we stop them from taking the trailer-Mog!"

"Why?" asked the colonel and professor together.

"Remember the quantum encryption we built into the software that controls de-Mogging?"

"Yes," said the colonel. "That's to keep anyone from being able to guess the command signal for de-Mogging the RoboBattlePets. You told us the encryption code was unbreakable, right? So even if they take the Mog, they won't be able to figure out the de-Mogging command."

"It *is* unbreakable when implemented properly," said Dad quickly. "But when I was debugging the software for the stadium de-Mogging system, I found a coding error, a bug. It's *not* implemented properly. If the Squiddies get access to the current software in any of our de-Moggers, then they'll be able learn our encryption technique, break our code, and de-Mog our RoboBattlePets before we can fire a shot!"

"But can't we just change the command signal or the encryption code?" suggested Sofie.

"No." Dad shook his head. "Once they learn our encryption technique, then their computers are powerful enough to break whatever code we pick. We have to stop them from taking the Mog!"

"But they're not taking one of the remotes or one of the stadium de-Mogging computers," said Otto. "They're taking the trailer-Mog."

"The trailer-Mog *has* a de-Mog command transmitter built into it," said Dad wringing his hands. "I added it as an extra safety precaution in case a RoboBattlePet began misbehaving right after transforming." Otto suddenly remembered when Dad pushed the yellow button to de-Mog Doppler before the first college tournament.

"Look!" Carrie called out. President Providence had made a run for it. But once he got out of the shadow of the trailer-Mog, the green light grabbed him and he too was floating up toward the Squiddy ship. "They have the president!"

"I have a clear shot," said Otto as he slewed RoboTwo-Toe's plasma rifles toward the pod.

"No," cried Professor Kyoto, "you might hit the president!"

"But we have to do something," argued Sofie. "That tractor beam thing must be outside the ship's force field. We can probably blast it."

The president and the trailer-Mog floated higher.

"We have to stop them," agreed Colonel Santiago. "We can't risk the Squiddies getting the de-Mogging command code."

"But Daniel, we can't ask these children to go into battle and risk their lives again," argued Professor Kyoto.

"You're right," sighed Colonel Santiago. "Martin, can you command any of these RoboBattlePets?"

"Two-Toe would probably obey me."

"But I'm a way better shot than you are," argued Otto. "I always beat you at video games."

The president and trailer-Mog rose higher still.

"He's right," admitted Dad. He turned to Professor Kyoto. "Sarah, we have to stop them. And these kids are the best chance we've got."

"Don't worry, Professor," said Otto with a bravado he didn't feel. "We've done this kind of thing before."

Reluctantly, Professor Kyoto agreed.

Inside the green cone, the president was trying to get out of the beam, flapping his arms like a bird and kicking his legs.

"Otto," said Colonel Santiago. "Target the pod. On my command—"

But before he could give the order to fire, RoboTracy reared up, and squirted a long sticky strand of silk at the president.

"Tracy!" yelled Sofie. "What are you doing?"

The silk hit the president and stuck to his chest and arms. The hungry caterpillar sucked in the slack, and the silk rope went taut. The president stopped floating higher.

"Good job Tracy!" said Carrie. "Sofie, can you pull him out of the beam?"

"We'll try." Sofie commanded RoboTracy to back up, but the caterpillar's feet just slipped on the grass. "No. But at least he's not going any higher." The president floated in place like a kite on a string, while the trailer-Mog rose ever closer to the ship. Realizing what was happening, the president grabbed the silk cord and tried to pull himself along it.

A yellow beam of light from the pod swept over Otto and the group behind him.

"They know we're here," said Sofie ominously.

"Otto, on my command," said the colonel. "Everyone else, get back, and take cover."

Otto lined up the tractor beam pod in his targeting display.

"Otto," said Colonel Santiago, "Fire!"

Otto pulled his hand controller triggers. RoboTwo-Toe's plasma rifles fired, sending two blindingly white plasma bolts at the pod. They exploded on impact, and the pod rocked back and forth from the blast. The cone of green light also rocked back and forth, and the trailer-Mog with it.

Otto fired again, tracking the pod as it swung side to side. His hopes for an easy victory rose when he thought he saw signs of damage to the pod. In horror, he realized it was just the glowing red spot that had destroyed the shed. Before he could command RoboTwo-Toe to run, a red energy beam shot out from the spot. The beam hit Otto square in his saddle shield, knocking him and RoboTwo-Toe backward into the others behind them. The beam ricocheted off his shield and struck the stands next to them. The stands exploded in a shower of burning wood and steel.

Everyone scattered. RoboTwo-Toe scrambled to his feet and bolted away. Stunned, Otto fought down the panic rising in him. That weapon was much more powerful than the ion cannons the RoboClones had carried! He was lucky it had hit his saddle shield. If it had hit RoboTwo-Toe, he'd probably have de-Mogged.

"Two-Toe, go left, go left!" Otto tried to assess the tactical situation as they circled back around. Professor Kyoto had gathered kids and pets and was leading them toward the school at a run. Colonel Santiago and Dad were still crouching behind the blasted stands with the soldiers, including the wounded ones. Juanita was also there, curled in a ball on the ground next to Mr. London and clutching her kitten Binky.

Carrie and Ace charged off on their RoboBattlePets in different directions, their weapons firing at the pod. RoboTracy had let out more silk and managed to back up around the corner of the smoldering stands. She and Sofie were out of the line of fire but still tugging tightly on the silk rope attached to the president.

The red dot on the pod fired a shot at Ace, but RoboNapoleon had just turned. The red bolt of energy missed, blowing a crater in the ground behind them. While Ace drew its fire, Carrie and Otto unloaded on the pod, being careful not to hit the president.

"Keep moving," yelled Otto to Carrie. She commanded RoboCookies to the side—just as the pod blasted a crater in the ground right where they had been.

While RoboTwo-Toe ran away from the blasted crater, Otto swung his cannons, took careful aim, and fired another plasma blast. The pod swung again from the hit but still appeared undamaged.

"Hard right!" he commanded, just before the pod fired back, blasting a crater behind them.

Ace turned RoboNapoleon toward the saucer, galloped straight at it, and fired. *No!* thought Otto. *Running straight at the pod will make them too easy of a target!* The pod fired and blasted RoboNapoleon with a direct hit. There was a flash, and RoboNapoleon turned back into a normal horse. Otto was amazed to see Ace fall a few feet and land sitting on Napoleon's bare back. Ace threw his arms around the horse's neck and they galloped away.

Otto heard Carrie yelling at the pod as she fired on it to draw its attention away from Ace and Napoleon. The red dot turned back toward Carrie, who urged RoboCookies to start running. His robotic leg exoskeletons propelled him quickly and let him turn nimbly as the pod blasted several craters around them.

But the situation was quickly growing more desperate. It was just Otto and Carrie left in the fight, and he didn't know how long they would last against the pod's powerful weapon. What was worse, the pod's aim seemed to be improving, perhaps learning from experience.

Otto fired another blast at the pod. "Hard left!" commanded Otto, and RoboTwo-Toe turned sharply. The pod fired, this time hitting the ground so close in front of them that RoboTwo-Toe stumbled and fell.

RoboTwo-Toe got up just in time for Otto to see RoboCookies take a direct hit. Amazingly, the tough beast did not de-Mog. The blast must have hit armor or Carrie's saddle shield, but RoboCookies was down and not getting up. The red dot on the pod swung back toward Otto.

"Hard right!" he commanded. The next blast missed just to their left.

Otto turned RoboTwo-Toe back toward the stands and was horrified to see Juanita chasing Binky out in the open. The kitten must have panicked. They were running straight at Otto. If Juanita was any closer to him the next time the pod fired at him, the blast might kill her!

"Hard left!" commanded Otto. A red bolt from the pod just missed him as they turned away from Juanita. The explosion knocked Juanita and Binky to the ground. She got to her hands and knees, apparently okay. But another blast soon drove RoboTwo-Toe back toward Juanita, who had picked up Binky and was holding the stunned kitten close to her chest. She stared wide-eyed as RoboTwo-Toe barreled down on her.

"Stop, Two-Toe!" shouted Otto, even though he knew that to stop would make them an easier target. But just as RoboTwo-Toe skidded to a halt, Ace galloped past on Napoleon and scooped up Juanita with one outstretched arm.

"Hard left!" commanded Otto to turn RoboTwo-Toe away from Ace. A red beam from the pod blasted a crater where Juanita had just been standing.

With Carrie down, RoboNapoleon de-Mogged, and Sofie behind the stands, it was just Otto and RoboTwo-Toe against the saucer. They were alone, just like when he was fighting a boss in a video game. Otto's mind slid into gaming mode. "Hard left."

RoboTwo-Toe zigged left. What was this boss's weakness? "Hard right." RoboTwo-Toe zagged right as another blast from the pod struck the ground. If he couldn't destroy the boss, was there another way to defeat him?

Of course! The trailer-Mog! But if he did that, would the president survive? Would the president survive if he didn't? Would Earth survive if the Squiddies learned how to de-Mog their RoboBattlePets?

Otto made his decision. He shifted his aim and—

He never saw the shot that hit them. All he noticed was a brief red glow. Time seemed to slow down as one of RoboTwo-Toe's plasma rifles exploded, taking a huge chunk out of the giant cat's shoulder. Otto's shocked mind noted numbly that the de-Mogging flash was much brighter than he had expected. The next instant, he was soaring through the air, tumbling slowly, end-over-end. He hit the ground hard on his back, knocking the wind out of him.

He lay still for a moment and watched Two-Toe in the distance. The cat was back to normal and running away as fast as he could. Through the haze of his shocked mind, the only thing he felt was relief that Two-Toe was okay.

The need to breathe finally forced him to remember where he was.

Pain and blind panic shot through Otto as he rolled over and crawled away from the saucer, gasping for breath. He felt absolutely naked and exposed. He was terrifyingly aware that there stood nothing between him and the Squiddy weapon. One shot meant certain death. In front of Otto was a blast crater. He scrambled frantically toward it, heaved himself over the raised rim, and slid down inside.

Otto curled up in a ball and tried to catch his breath. His ears were ringing, and he couldn't stop shaking. The smell of burnt grass and steaming dirt stung his nose. He longed desperately for the safety and power of his RoboBattlePet. How could he fight without Two-Toe?

Things were hopeless. Their RoboBattlePets were being picked off one by one. The soldiers were out of the fight. Otto felt like giving up. Tears began welling up in his eyes. All he wanted to do was squeeze them shut and pretend this wasn't happening. He wanted to be home with his Mom. He was just a kid. No one would fault him for just laying low until the battle was over. Maybe the Air Force jets would show up soon, or the Army with more RoboBattlePets.

But what if the Squiddies got away with the trailer-Mog? A horrible sense of dread of the Squiddies learning the de-Mogging command washed over Otto. If they could de-Mog all the Army's RoboBattlePets, then they were certain to launch another full scale invasion. Terrifying memories of RoboClones attacking his neighborhood during the war rushed through his mind. If he gave up now, then it could all happen again. And next time, without RoboBattlePets standing in their way, the Squiddies *would* win.

He had to keep fighting.

Otto forced his mind back to the present. He was alive. None of his bones were broken, and Two-Toe was safe. Those were all good things. Carrie and Sofie were still on their RoboBattlePets. Maybe he could still help them defeat the Squiddies.

Otto willed himself back into action and raised his eyes over the crater rim. The trailer-Mog was still rising within the green cone, and the president was still floating in place—held by RoboTracy's silk rope. The pod was no longer firing. Apparently, it didn't consider RoboTracy a threat. He looked over at Carrie.

Hope shot through him when he saw that RoboCookies was slowly getting back to his feet. Throwing caution to the wind, Otto scrambled up out of the crater and sprinted toward them.

"Carrie!" yelled Otto as soon as he got close enough for her to hear. "Shoot the Mog! Shoot the trailer-Mog!"

Carrie looked at him, nodded, and turned her attention to her targeting display.

Otto dove to the ground and sprawled flat as RoboCookie's phaser blasters fired.

The phaser beams hit the trailer-Mog.

It exploded in a strange way, as if the green tractor beam contained it somewhat.

But the explosion seemed to temporarily disrupt the cone of green light. In that instant, the blast, combined with the pull of RoboTracy's silk rope, propelled President Providence out of the green cone.

Several small pieces of the trailer-Mog also flew out, but most of them still hung inside the green tractor-beam. The president fell to the ground in a crumpled heap.

Suddenly, the green cone of light shut off, and the smoldering remnants of the trailer-Mog fell to the ground, just missing the president, who was being pulled along the ground as RoboTracy sucked in the silk cord. The red light on the pod faded away, and the pod began rising toward the saucer as its cable retracted.

As the pod neared the bottom of the saucer, Otto could see the shimmering of the spaceship's force field opening to allow the pod to pass through. *That's just like in Scandinavian Smackdown IV when the souls passed through the Giant King's magical force shield,* thought Otto. Sneaking an arrow through the shield along with the soul was the only way to defeat the final boss.

"Carrie!" he yelled again. "Fire at the edge of the pod!"

She fired. One phaser beam struck the edge of the pod, but a second beam skimmed past the pod, slipped inside the force field, and struck the saucer with a small explosion. The spaceship listed to one side and then accelerated quickly back the way it had come, its force field flickering and making a crackling sound.

The roar of two fighter jets passing overhead startled Otto. The fighters each fired a missile at the Squiddy spaceship. The first missile exploded on the ship's force field, which winked out. The second missile then struck the saucer. The Squiddy ship listed further, trailing smoke. The saucer fired red beams at the jets as they circled around for another pass, but the aliens missed. The jets closed in behind the saucer as all three craft disappeared over the horizon.

Otto stood up and took a few deep breaths as the adrenaline drained from his body. His head hurt, and so did his back. But he didn't care. They were alive, and the Squiddies didn't have the de-Mogging code.

Anxiously, he scanned the grounds between him and the parking lot. His heart leapt when he saw Two-Toe sitting on the hood of a car, licking his paw as if nothing had happened. Otto ran over and picked up Two-Toe. He held the cat close as he walked over to the blasted stands. Two-Toe's purring helped calm Otto down. Carrie and RoboCookies caught up to him just as he reached the stands. Ace rode up on Napoleon from another part of the field. Juanita sat behind him, one arm tightly around his waist, the other holding Binky, who looked fine.

Dad, Sofie, and Colonel Santiago were tending to President Providence. He was sitting up and leaning against RoboTracy while Colonel Santiago finished putting one of his arms in a makeshift sling. Otto was glad to see that RoboTracy hadn't eaten President Providence. The president looked a bit singed and sooty, but otherwise okay. He gave them a shell-shocked smile as they arrived.

"Carrie, you blew up the trailer-Mog!" exclaimed Dad suddenly.

"I'm sorry," said Carrie defensively. "It was Otto's idea."

"Nice going, Otto," said Sofie, shaking her head.

Otto couldn't believe it. They had just defeated the Squiddies, and he was in trouble?

"But there was no other option—" Otto stopped as Sofie smirked.

"No," smiled Colonel Santiago while Sofie laughed, "that was a brilliant tactical move! We're very proud of you. We're proud of all of you." He beamed at them.

Ace and Juanita climbed off of Napoleon. Juanita threw her arms around Ace's neck. "You're my hero!" she cried and hugged him hard. Carrie looked quite annoyed as Ace awkwardly patted Juanita's back.

"Where's everyone else?" asked Carrie, looking away from Ace and Juanita.

"Over there." Sofie pointed to where Professor Kyoto, Mr. London, and some of the soldiers were walking over from the school, leading the rest of the kids and their pets. Two soldiers were supporting Mr. London.

Randy looked pretty beat up. He was covered in dirt and scratches, and his left arm was in a sling. He sat down gingerly away from the others, wrapped his good arm around his legs, and rested his head on his knees. The rest of the group looked a bit dirty but uninjured, except for Darrell who had a bandage on his forehead where a piece of the exploding stands had struck him.

President Providence stood up with Dad's help. "Kids, I was wrong. I've changed my mind about the Junior League. I feel safer knowing that you're helping the military defend us against the Squiddies."

"So we get to have the Junior League after all!" squealed Carrie.

"Yes," the president said.

All the kids cheered.

"But we will need to improve our safety procedures," said Professor Kyoto. "And I think many of you need to do a better job training your pets."

"Randy," said Mr. London pompously. "You need to get that dog of yours trained better or you're off the team! Do you realize—"

"Mr. London," interrupted Professor Kyoto. "I'm sure Randy understands the importance of training his dog better. Perhaps we should have some more pet training clinics before we have another practice."

Randy just stared at the ground in silence. Conan came close and licked his face.

"Are you okay, Randy?" asked Professor Kyoto kindly.

"I'll be fine," said Randy glumly as he patted Conan. He got up and began walking away.

"Where're you going?" asked Carrie as she climbed off RoboCookies.

Randy stopped and turned. "The library. I want to get a book on dog training."

"That's a great idea," said Professor Kyoto. "But you need to wait for the medics to check out that arm."

Military trucks and tanks were already rumbling into the parking lot. Behind them came ambulances and news crew vans.

"I could help you train Conan not to chase cats," offered Carrie.

"Really?" said Randy hopefully. "You'd do that?"

"Sure. We can start tomorrow, if you want."

"Okay," said Randy, nodding. "Thanks."

Several medics arrived and began tending to the injured. One of them checked out Otto and cleaned some scrapes he hadn't noticed in all the excitement.

"Martin, I need you to get that laboratory Mog back online as soon as possible," said Colonel Santiago as he watched several fighter jets patrolling the sky. "We may still need it today."

"Right," said Dad. The colonel nodded and strode toward the arriving military vehicles.

"I'll stay here with the children," said Professor Kyoto.

"Okay," said Dad. "Carrie, Sofie, I need to de-Mog your RoboBattlePets before I get to work on the Mog."

"But I wanted to see if Tracy can catch chipmunks with that silk-spitting trick of hers. Could I please?" asked Sofie hopefully.

"Not today," said Dad. He raised his remote and de-Mogged RoboCookies. Sofie climbed down off of RoboTracy and then Dad de-Mogged her as well. Several of the other kids were on their multi-comms talking to their parents. While Dad called home to let Mom know that they were all okay, Ace came over and said goodbye to Carrie. He was going to ride Napoleon home while his father rode to the hospital in an ambulance.

"I want you three with me," Dad told his children as he closed his multi-comm. Otto and his sisters walked with him toward the lab, with Two-Toe and Doppler trotting along behind them.

"Dad, when are the wrist-Mogs going to be ready?" asked Sofie.

"I should have a prototype in about a month."

"Cool," said Otto. That eased his mind a bit. He wanted to forget about the Squiddies for a while and think about more pleasant things, like the Junior League. But suddenly he remembered something that was bothering him. "Carrie!" Otto blurted in disgust. "I can't believe you're going to help Randy."

"We've got a second chance to make the Junior League a success," lectured Carrie. "So we all need to work together, even if we're not on the same team, or even if we don't all like each other."

"Okay, good point," grumbled Otto. Carrie was right. The Squiddies were the real enemy. Otto was willing to do anything he could to defeat them. But he had to admit, he really wanted to beat Randy and Team London in a tournament. He figured that was okay, though, because the whole point of the Junior League was to let competition drive them to create the best RoboBattlePet designs.

"Dad, when we get to the lab, can I use the design system?"

"Sure."

"Thanks." Now that he had seen RoboConan in action, Otto had a few ideas for improving his Arctic Panther design to get the upper hand.

He couldn't wait until the next practice!

CPSIA information can be obtained at www.ICGtesting.com
Printed in the USA
LVOW061204301011

252706LV00002B/136/P